Susanna

Hits HOLLYWOOD

by

MARY HOGAN

To my very own Hollywood hottie . . .
you know who you are.

SIMON AND SCHUSTER
First published in Great Britain in 2007
by Simon & Schuster UK Ltd
A CBS COMPANY

3 5 7 9 10 8 6 4 2

Simon & Schuster UK Ltd
Africa House
64–78 Kingsway
London WC2B 6AH

A CIP catalogue record for this book is
available from the British Library.

ISBN-13: 978-1-4169-0158-7

Set in 12/17.75 pt Adobe Garamond by
Rowland Phototypesetting Ltd, Bury St Edmunds, Suffolk
Printed and bound in Great Britain by Cox & Wyman, Reading, Berkshire

ACKNOWLEDGEMENTS

Gigantic thanks to Natalie Vo and the Press Office staff at the gorgeous Kodak Theatre for giving me a private tour and behind-the-scenes peek at the centre of Oscar-night action. A huge thank-you also to Rosemary Lovejoy of American Airlines for letting me lounge in the Admiral's Club like a Hollywood star.

I've been lucky to have *two* amazing editors on this book. Thank you both, Venetia Gosling and Joanna Moult, for helping shape and refine our Susanna so beautifully. Also, my gratitude and admiration go out to publicist extraordinare Penelope Webber for taking me all around the UK without once losing patience or cheerfulness.

Finally, my agent Laura Langlie is quite simply, the *best*. 'Nuf said.

ONE

This *cannot* be happening to me. The Trips – my three baby bros – are tripping *out*. Sam is wearing a bowl of apple sauce on his head. Evan's just sat on his sagging, stinking diaper and shoved a Cheerio up his nose. Henry heard Oprah say, 'Thanks so much!' on the TV and now he's repeating it over and over with a lisp.

'Thank*th tho* mu*tth*.'

'Mom!' I shout. Though I know she can't hear me. She's taking one of her marathon showers. Not that I blame her. I'd lock myself in the bathroom, too, if I had two-year-old triplets, and one of them had a loaded diaper toxic enough to melt the tattoos off Tommy Lee.

At this particular time, however, I don't care that my mother needs a moment to herself. Do *my* needs count for nothing? Isn't a mother supposed to be there for her off-spring? Even if, as she told me, 'My hair is full of spit-up and my deodorant stopped working three days ago.' She didn't reek *that* bad, and I need her now. *Right* now. Nell

1

Wickham – the glamorous whack-job editor of *Scene* magazine, a woman obsessed with her pores, her carbs, her reign as celebrity Buzz Queen, a Brit who brought me into her queendom last summer as a teen intern and taught me everything a good servant should know – just rang from the lobby of our building to say she's on her way up.

Good God, is that a slice of pizza upside-down on the floor?

'Thank*th tho*—'

'Henry! Go play with Pooh Bear!' I say, turning off the television and shoving my dirty socks under the couch cushions. Then my eyes dart over to the window in our train wreck of an apartment. Suddenly, it seems like a brilliant idea to dash five flights down the fire escape and run off through the icy streets of New York City barefoot. What's a little frostbite, and a night spent in a psychiatric facility for observation, when one of the most stylish women on this side of the Atlantic is about to see the pathetic state of my home life?

Nell knocks on the door. Hard.

It's no use. She knows I'm here. She already heard me ask, 'Who is it?' over the intercom when she rang our apartment. Which is one of the few things that sucks about living in New York. You can't peer through your curtains, see your boss pull into the driveway, and hide

2

behind the couch. I guess you could refuse to *ever* answer the intercom buzzer, but then you'd never get packages from UPS or flowers from your boyfriend. Not that I have a boyfriend. If I did, I'd definitely answer the door. Just in case.

Hearing the knock, Henry screams, '*Th*anta Cla*wth*?'

My heart is thudding. Frantically, I smooth my straggly hair. It's normally curly, chest-length and chestnut brown. At this moment, it's flat, shoulder-length, and the colour of mud. There's no time to change out of my sweatpants, either. Taking a deep breath, I attempt a model*esque* indifference as I open the door and face the woman who made my life a living hell last summer.

'Oh, hi,' I say, casually.

'You don't,' Nell gasps, her British accent in full bellow.

'I don't what?'

'Have a lift.'

Poking my head outside the door, I see the 'Out of Service' notice taped to the elevator doors in our Super's illegible scrawl.

'Good news!' I chirp. 'You can skip the gym today.'

Nell growls. Without waiting to be invited in, she staggers past me. I feel the cold February air on the soft hair of her mink coat. I smell her customized perfume. The memories from last summer come flooding back. Instantly,

3

I'm the ugly stepsister trying to cram my humungous big toe into a pointy Manolo Blahnik glass slipper Nell pulled from the fashion closet. Shaking them off, I saunter into our apartment.

'Can I get you a drink?' I ask, breezily. 'Green tea?' I add, remembering her preference.

'Yes,' she says. 'Tea.' Then, she flops down on our couch.

'Ooh. *Th*oft.'

Sam appears at the edge of the couch and pets Nell's mink. She glares at him like he's a pit bull.

'Sam, go play with your brothers,' I command.

He doesn't budge. Instead, Evan toddles over, his lethal diaper now almost touching the floor. Evan now has *two* Cheerios up his nose – one for each nostril.

'*Th*ock,' he says, pulling one of my dirty white socks from beneath the couch cushion. Before I have a chance to grab it from him, Evan flings it at Nell's face. It lands diagonally across her blonde head, making her look like the walking wounded with a filthy home-made bandage wrapped around her skull. Evan and Sam erupt in hysterical laughter. It *is* funny. Especially when the Cheerios fly out of Evan's nose and land millimetres from Nell's gazillion-dollar mink. Sam's apple sauce bowl falls from his head and hits the floor with a *splat*.

Who knew my brothers were the Three Stooges reincarnated?

'Yo, Mom!' I call loudly, plucking the sock from Nell's head just as Evan pulls the other one out from the couch. Thankfully, I'm able to grab it before he throws.

'*Thockth*,' he squeals at me, reaching his hands in the air. Then my other two brothers do the same.

'*Thockth*!'

'*Thockth*!'

Since when do all three brothers lisp? Is it possible that three two-year-olds would conspire to deliberately make my family look like hillbillies in front of the terminally chic Nell Wickham?

'It's the nanny's day off,' I lie.

Smiling a fake smile, Nell removes Sam's hand from her mink and holds it up like a dead fish.

'Cute boys,' she says, unconvincingly. 'And so many of them.'

I'm tempted to explain how fertility treatments can sometimes go awry, and how three babies only *seem* like thirty, and how cute they are when they're running around the apartment naked after their baths, and how I *normally* wear really cool clothes after school, and how I have no idea how that slice of pizza ended up face-down on the floor.

5

Instead, forcing my voice to sound sunny, I ask, 'What brings you here this afternoon?'

Nell blinks. 'I have an appointment to meet your parents.'

'That's *tomorrow.*'

'Tomorrow?' Her left eyebrow arches.

'Yes. Carmen called last week to confirm.'

Nell sits up and gently shoves The Trips away from her coat. All three are now petting it.

She sighs. 'Carmen left for her holiday yesterday. I'm absolutely adrift without her.'

Adrift? You *adrift* yourself over here without giving me a chance to hide the chaos I live in?!

Expecting Nell to stand and sheepishly apologise for showing up on the wrong day, I step back. I give her room to rise up and sweep her minked self right out our front door and down the stairs. Instead, she stands and takes her coat *off*.

'On a padded hanger,' she says, handing it to me. 'Or wood.'

My mouth, I notice, is open. The Trips are now encircling me. Henry rests his head on Nell's mink and says, '*Th*leepy.'

'How's that tea coming, Susan?'

Behind Nell's back, I roll my eyes. Six months, and

6

nothing has changed. Nell still can't get my name right, I'm still her servant, and my continuing internship at *Scene* is still the best thing that's ever happened to me.

'Coming right up,' I say.

Nell moves down to the clean end of the couch and makes herself comfy.

Ha, ha! I say to myself on the way to the hall closet. There is no clean section of our couch!

'I smell poop, Susanna! Did you check the diapers?'

Building on the hillbilly theme, my mother – finally out of the shower – shouts from her bedroom. I half expect her to appear with a piece of straw hanging out her mouth and a blackened tooth.

'Poop!' Evan squeals joyfully, clapping his hands.

Her hair wrapped in a fraying towel, her body wrapped in my father's plaid flannel robe, Mom marches into the living room. Is it possible that I never noticed my mother wears mismatched slippers? One brown, one navy blue?

'Look who's come to tea,' I say.

'Oh, my,' Mom replies.

Nell rises and floats towards her.

'You must be Susan's mother,' Nell says, reaching both hands out.

I wait for my mom to tell her my name is Susan*na*, which Nell *knows*, but refuses to acknowledge for some insane, narcissistic reason, but Mom doesn't. She holds Dad's robe closed with one hand, and shakes Nell's hand with the other.

'Nell's a day early,' I say. Though it's like, *so* obvious.

'My secretary is on holiday and I'm deaf, dumb and blind without her,' Nell says. 'Can you ever forgive me for popping in like this?'

No, I want to say firmly, we can't.

My mother springs into action. 'Don't worry about a thing, Nell. We're happy to have you any time. Have a seat. Make yourself at home. Give me two minutes to get dressed. Susanna, hang up Nell's coat and put the kids in the playpen in the bedroom.'

Whirling around, my mother disappears. Nell sits as I hang her coat over my down jacket. The closest we come to a padded hanger. I then herd my three brothers into the back bedroom.

'Back in a moment,' Henry says to Nell, in a freakishly perfect imitation of Oprah Winfrey.

When I come back into the living room, Nell has draped herself elegantly on the couch and my mother is heating the kettle on the stove. Somehow, Mom even picked up the pizza slice and cleaned the apple sauce blob and Cheerios. I've never loved her more in my life.

'We simply adored having Susan work with us at

Scene last summer,' Nell says when Mom joins her. I sit across from Nell and stare, remembering how they actually adored my ability to carry six venti skim lattes into a staff meeting without dropping any Splenda sweetener packets. Not to mention assuring Nell that her freshly collagened lips didn't look like two water balloons – which they did – and wrestling a cockroach the size of a small pony – which it was. Ah, but who can forget how I, Susanna Barringer – budding celebrity reporter extra-ordinaire – wrangled an invite to Randall Sanders' (sigh) movie premiere? So what if life in celebville turned out to be different than I expected? I happen to know that life in Nellville is pure *fantasy*land. Like her delusion last summer that Vince Vaughn might fall for her. Dream on! From Jen to Nell? Nell is hot enough for a middle-aged stick figure, but I totally lied about not seeing her pores.

'The trip to Los Angeles will be a great opportunity for our girl,' Nell continues.

I smile, toss my hair and attempt to style my sweats by raising one elastic leg up to my knee.

'She'll be working with our photographer, Keith Franklin.'

My heart flutters at the mention of Keith's name. Keith Franklin and Randall Sanders at the same event? I should get an Oscar for acting cool around two of the hottest hotties ever.

Before Nell has the chance to gaze down at my bare feet and shriek, I hide my need for a pedi by curling my toes under my feet. It hurts like mad, and looks like the result of a spinal cord injury, but I know Nell – she'd rather I was mangled than badly groomed.

'Sue is a valued member of the *Scene* team,' Nell says.

I blush and tuck my ragged fingernails out of sight, too.

Mom says, 'I have a few concerns.'

Instantly, Nell spits out, 'Of course, we'll get someone else if you have reservations.'

Someone else?! Are you off your trolley! I've been looking forward to this trip since last summer! How many fifteen-year-old New York high-schoolers get the chance to fly to California to cover the Academy Awards for *Scene* magazine?! Well, not *cover* exactly. More like *assist*. Probably, a lot like assist in getting venti skim lattes without dropping any Splenda packets. But, who cares! The Academy Awards! A valued member of the *Scene* team! A weekend in Hollywood! Working with Keith Franklin. The chance to see stars! Leo, Orlando, Keira! Maybe even (double sigh) the Randy Man himself. Will he remember me? Will he say hello from the red carpet? Will Ran—

'Well, Susanna?'

Mom and Nell are staring at me. I haven't heard a word they've said.

'Hmm,' I say, trying to look thoughtful.

Mom says, 'If you have to think about it, I can't let you go.'

'Yes! Yes! The answer is yes!'

'Yes?' Mom is incredulous. 'You'll have trouble catching up on your schoolwork if I let you take Monday off.'

'No!' I leap to my unpedicured feet. 'It's all planned out. My teachers know about it. I'm doing extra credit. It's only one school day. I'll be fine.'

The kettle whistles. Nell asks, 'Actually, do you have white tea, Susie? With low-carb honey?'

Reluctant to leave my mother alone with the woman who outed me as a virgin at a staff meeting, I walk my feet into the kitchen, but leave my ears in the living room.

'I promise to take good care of her,' I hear Nell say. Yeah right, I laugh. Nell can't even take care of an *appointment*.

Turning off the whistling kettle, and searching through our tea bag selection, I see black, green, orange pekoe. Is white tea just black tea with tons of milk? Do they even make low-carb honey? Are the bees genetic mutants?

Through the open archway between our kitchen and

the living room, I hear my mother give the final okay for my trip. Whew! In three days, I'll be jetting off to the coast to assist *Scene*'s dreamy photographer, Keith Franklin, with the most exciting event of the year. I can take care of myself.

'Never mind about the tea, Susan,' Nell calls into the kitchen, standing. 'I'd better get back to the office. I have a faint memory that I'm supposed to meet with Jack Black's manager. Or, is it Jack *Nicholson's*?'

Mom laughs. But, of course, Nell is serious.

'A driver will pick you up early Saturday morning,' Nell says to me before leaving. 'Remember to bring light clothes. It's seventy degrees out there.'

My whole body tingles. *Hollywood*. Oscar night. How lucky can a girl get?

'I'll be ready,' I say.

I've been ready to show the world what I can do all my life.

TWO

The alarm rings at five in the morning. Not that I need an alarm clock. I'm totally awake. I hardly slept at all last night. In fact, it still *looks* like night in my bedroom. The air vibrates with night-time particles. The silence is both eerie and exhilarating, like I'm in some forbidden time zone between two days.

Quickly, I put on the clothes I laid out last night.

Ping!

My computer lets me know I have an instant message. Of course, I know who it is.

'U up?' I type.

'No,' Amelia types back.

I laugh. She writes, 'Kiss Jake G 4 me?'

'If I must.'

'U MUST!'

Since last summer, Mel – my smart, kind, volunteers-to-cheer-up-terminally-ill-patients best friend – has worked up a healthy celebrity obsession. Nothing like mine, of course. It takes *years* of studying *Entertainment Tonight* and *E! True Hollywood Story* to create a proper star-fixation. But she's coming along nicely. Last year she would have asked me to kiss the Surgeon General for her. Not that I ever would.

'Luv U,' I type.

'DTO.'

'CYA.'

We sign off just as my dad pokes his head through my doorway.

'Scrambled eggs?' he asks, yawning.

I smile. Everything you need to know about my father is contained in those two words. *Scrambled eggs.* Though The Trips wipe him out, he's up before dawn to make me breakfast. Dad always makes a supreme effort to remind me of the good old days when I was my parents' one and only. He works crazy hours in a creepy job that is now cool, but is still creepy if you know the reality. Dad is a forensic scientist . . . not to be confused with a Hollywood-created CSI – a crime scene investigator, made popular by the glut of CSI spin-offs on TV. In real life, guys like my dad spend most of their time peering into microscopes and digging through other people's trash for used Kleenex and other gross stuff that might have DNA smeared on it. Plus, no offence to my dad, but he wears nerdy glasses and has greyish hair and the evidence of too many pasta dinners around his middle. I've been to his lab, too. *Nobody* wears low-cut tank tops and tight jeans. They look more like Marge Simpson than Marg Helgenberger. And don't get me started about David Caruso on the Miami version. What's up with his sunglasses fetish? He spends the whole show dramatically putting them on and taking them off!

'Or orange juice?' Dad asks.

That's the real CSI – a man who gets up in the dark to make his daughter scrambled eggs and orange juice before heading uptown on the subway to his basement office next to the morgue. Honestly, even on the hottest day in summer, I've never seen my dad in shades.

'No thanks,' I say to my father, hastily making my bed. 'I'm too excited to eat. Besides, they'll serve breakfast on the plane, won't they? Our flight leaves at seven-thirty.'

Dad says, 'Don't count on food. Unless you're in first class.'

Flipping my hair, I say, 'Of course I'll be in first class. Would Nell Wickham ever fly with the riff-raff?'

He chuckles as he grabs my suitcase and carries it to the front door. I tiptoe down the hall and poke my head through my parents' open bedroom doorway.

'Don't forget to wear sunscreen,' Mom says, groggily, her head sticking out of the covers.

'I'll miss you, too,' I reply, smiling.

Propping herself up on her elbows, Mom says, 'Your father and I are incredibly proud of you, Susanna.'

My hand flies up to my chest. I feel my heart pumping into my palm. 'Thanks, Mom,' I say, my voice quivering. Especially since I know that she thinks flying to Hollywood to cover the red carpet is as trivial as mourning Hilary and Chad's break-up and celebrating Paris and Nicole's. Though I hear Paris and Nicole have hugged and made up – or are they cat-fighting again? Plus, she's *horrified* that one of my all-time fav shows is *Taxicab Confessions,* where they hide a cam in a New York City cab and tape passengers doing and saying seriously racy and raunchy stuff. My dad agrees with my mom. He's convinced my brain will shrivel to the size of a raisin if I continue to fill it with what he calls 'drivel'.

'Have you ever thought about exploring the Universe instead of the love life of stars?' he once asked me.

'Can you believe how incredibly cute Ashton Holmes is?' I replied.

Mom rolls over in her bed. 'I'm not kidding about sunscreen, Susanna,' she says, yawning. 'You know how I feel about tans.'

'I know.'

My mother views a tan as 'skin damage', which, of

16

course, it is. Which is why my legs look like two pieces of chalk.

'I will return as pale and virginal as the day I left you,' I say. Though I think, 'Unless Randall Sanders scoops me into his arms and whisks me off to his Hollywood mansion. In that case, I'll return pale and grinning from ear to ear.'

'Say hi to Nell for me,' Mom says. 'And tell her I've gotten a new robe.'

'But, you haven't.'

'I haven't lost my baby belly, either. Does she need to know everything?'

I laugh and kiss my mother goodbye.

Shutting my parents' bedroom door behind me, I continue creeping quietly down the hallway in our apartment. The wood floorboards creak, but no way am I flying three thousand miles without saying goodbye to my brothers. Risky as it is.

The door squeaks like a trapped kitten as I push it open. Inside, in the green glow of the night-light, I see three cribs and hear the sounds of three babies breathing peacefully. Evan has his mouth open in a perfect little 'O'. Henry and Sam both sleep with their tiny hands curled beneath their chins. I nearly burst into tears, they're so cute. Until Sam suddenly opens his eyes.

Uh-oh.

'Hey, Sammy,' I whisper. His hair feels like a feather duster – all thin and soft. 'Go back to sleep.'

Sam blinks. He stretches his arms up to me. I know what that means.

'I can't hold you right now,' I whisper. 'I'm on my way to Hollywood.'

Clearly, Sam has no interest in my budding career as a celebrity reporter. He simply opens his mouth and starts to cry.

'Shhhh,' I begin, gently rubbing his belly. But it's no use. Once Sam gets going, Henry and Evan soon follow. In unison, they open their eyes, grunt, gurgle, then release two full-on wails.

'Oops,' I say to my dad when he appears in the doorway.

He sighs. 'No big deal, Susanna. They were going to be up in two or three hours anyway.'

It's dark and cold outside. Our block is deserted and the streetlights are still on. My nose instantly runs. I'm dressed for California – jeans, a long-sleeved T-shirt, sneakers – and my feet are freezing on the icy New York sidewalk.

Beep. Beep.

Across the street, an idling black sedan honks its horn.

The windows are fogged. White steams billows from the exhaust pipe. As I drag my suitcase over a hardened mound of dirty snow, the driver pops the trunk and gets out of the car.

'I'll take that,' he says, reaching for my suitcase. 'Hop in.'

'Do you have a pick-up name?'

I'm a New Yorker. No way am I going to hop in just *any* black sedan!

'Susan? Sue? Suzanne? It's written on my schedule in the front seat.'

'Close enough,' I say, shivering. Then I hand him my suitcase, and circle around to sit in the back seat.

'Keith!' I squeal. 'I didn't know yo—'

'I was out till one-thirty last night. I haven't had coffee yet, and the headache behind my right eyeball feels like a pushpin. Can we do our meet and greet later?'

'Of course!' I chirp, my *voice* a pushpin.

'You might want to shut the door, Susanna. It's freezing.'

Keith winces as I slam the car door. He then lowers his eyelids and leans his gorgeous head against the window.

'Wake me at the airport,' he mumbles.

'Will do!' Now I wince. Will I *ever* not be a total doof

around a guy whose cheekbones make me go weak at the knees?

'Ready?' the driver asks me as he stares in his rear-view mirror.

Clamping my mouth shut, I flash a thumbs-up. The driver pulls away from the kerb and we're on our way. My amazing adventure has officially begun. For the next three days, I, Susanna Barringer, will have the chance to show the world (okay, not the *world*, but Nell and Keith and the snarky fashion editor, Sasha) that I am one of them. A member of the *Scene* magazine team. I have three days to prove that I'm more than a mere teen intern – more than a celeb-obsessed high-schooler who is very possibly in *way* over her head.

THREE

New York's Hudson River is slate grey in the dim morning light. As we drive down the West Side Highway, I wipe frost off the window and watch the city wake up. A garbage truck rumbles down a side street. A man in a green uniform tosses salt chunks on the sidewalk to soak up the ice. By the time we reach lower Manhattan, the Statue of Liberty is a shimmering sliver of golden light.

Keith sleeps the whole way. Handy for me because I find myself studying him the way an art dealer studies a rare painting. This is how he looks when he rolls out of bed!? Hung-over? Like me, Keith has curly hair. Sadly, that's where our similarities end. He's *way* prettier than I am. Keith's hair is almost black and his curls have a sexy tousled look. My brown hair changes with the weather. Flat curls in winter, frizz in summer, flyaway in high heat and totally lopsided if I sleep on one side. Which I do every night.

Grunting slightly, Keith turns his head towards the

window. A curl falls past his closed left eye, mingling with his long, black lashes. I'm tempted to reach over and return the curl to his scrumptious head, but I don't want to risk waking him. I do, however, long to touch the stubble on his Adam's apple and run my finger across his cherry-coloured lips to see if they're as soft as they look.

After forty minutes of intense observation, I still can't see a flaw. What must it feel like to walk through life with a perfect face? If I see Johnny Depp on the red carpet, I'll be sure to ask him.

'We're here,' I say, gently shaking Keith awake.

JFK airport is crawling with sleepy people. Instantly, I notice that travelling with Keith Franklin, the star photog of *Scene* magazine, is nothing like travelling with my family. When the Barringer Bunch – as Dad loves to call us – goes anywhere, it's a mess of car seats, stinky cabs, long lines and horrified faces when passengers realise my three brothers are sitting next to them. Today, everything is different.

Keith rolls his carry-on bag straight past the line at the ticket counter. I follow behind him, rolling my own suitcase and carrying his camera bags on my shoulder. We go up an escalator, down an empty hallway, and through a frosted-glass door with an emblem that reads 'Admiral's Club'. The inner sanctum. Where the rich and famous check in and wait for their planes so they don't have to sit with people like me. My heart flutters. Will I snag a celebrity scoop before I even leave New York? Will Britney be inside with a mess of car seats?

The Admiral's Club is nothing like any waiting room I've ever seen. Number one: it's silent. The only sounds are the crinkling of *Wall Street Journals* and the faint drone of CNN. Leather chairs are separated by tall plants and short coffee tables. We pass a counter full of bagels and glasses of orange juice. Number two: they're all *free*.

I spot Nell ahead, stretched out on a leather recliner, behind large black sunglasses. Though she's clearly asleep, or pretending to be, I'm reluctant to walk past her. The smell of my drugstore shampoo may jolt her awake.

'What is that awful stench?' she'll ask, lifting her black glasses and glaring in my direction. 'Quick! Someone rewash Susan in Sisley Botanical!'

Thankfully, Nell doesn't move. And Keith grabs a recliner far enough away from her to be out of nose – or any other sensory – detection.

'We don't need to be at the gate for another half an hour,' Keith says. 'Wake me up, okay?'

Just like that, Keith settles in for another nap. Briefly, I consider napping next to him. It's definitely the closest we'll ever get to sleeping together. But who can sleep when you're in the 'royalty' room? If I hang out by the bagels, will Charlotte Church walk by?

Tucking the camera bags beneath Keith's chair, I make the most of my free half-hour. This is, after all, a flight from New York City to the celebrity capital of the world. On *Oscar* weekend. If Nell Wickham is asleep on a recliner, perhaps Tom and Katie are, too. Though, Tom, of course, would be *jumping* on it.

Last summer, when I was Nell's servile toady, my one afternoon with Keith Franklin taught me well. Stars can run, but they can't hide. So I scan the room for the celebrity *uniform*: hat (usually baseball cap, but not always), huge black sunglasses (even – especially! – indoors), baggy clothes to hide their professionally trained bodies and *Botoxia* – curiously dead upper lips.

The early-morning sun streaks through the huge windows as I make my way in and out of the various sections of the large private waiting room. I see men in suits on cells, women in black on laptops, and *lots* of surgically enhanced boobs. (Do they think those cantaloupes look real?) I also nearly faint when I see Toby Richmond, the actor who played the bad guy in Randall Sanders' last movie, *The Man in the Window*. Really, I almost *do* faint because I gasp when I turn the corner and see him, then forget to breathe.

He looks up just as I start coughing.

'Are you all right?'

I nod, cough again. Then I grab a *Wall Street Journal* and sit in an armchair across from him.

My heart is thumping. My ears feel hot.

How cool is this? Not even seven a.m. and I already have a celebrity sighting! One who *talked* to me! Toby played a creep whose hard life made him evil. The make-up artist put a nasty scar on his cheek, which looked sexy in a Seal sort of way. Now, with his feet propped up on a leather duffel bag and a BlackBerry on his lap, I'm dying to tell him how awful he was in the movie. Which, of course, means he's a great actor since he was *supposed* to be hateful.

Suddenly, Toby looks up, catches me staring. Again, I cough into my hand.

'Susanna, you idiot!' I screech to myself. 'Who wants to talk to a girl with Ebola?'

Quickly, I scan the newspaper for an appropriate conversation-starter.

'Will Bush ever learn?' I'll say, chuckling.

Toby will ask, 'What did he do now? Massage another world leader's shoulders?'

I'll toss my hair and giggle. Then, oh so casually, I'll move to the seat beside him, gush over his performance in *The Man in the Window* and pummel him for a scoop about my all-time favourite actor, Randall Sanders.

Sweet!

My plan quickly tanks. There is absolutely nothing to chuckle over. What's wrong with this paper? It's all bad news!

Frantically, I search for a dog rescue from a frozen lake or an ice sculpture of the mayor – anything to launch a conversation with Toby Richmond. Maybe the Sports sect—

'Toby!'

Sasha – the tall, stunning, excruciatingly thin fashion editor for *Scene* magazine – swoops into the room, throws herself on Toby's lap, and kisses him squarely on the lips. Is she squishing his BlackBerry? I wonder. Then I realise Sasha is so light she could sit on a *blueberry* without staining her dress.

'You always did know how to make an entrance,' Toby says, hugging her.

'I haven't seen you in ages,' Sasha coos. 'You look unbelievably yummy.'

'You're yummier.' Toby snuggles Sasha's neck.

'Are you a presenter?' she asks.

'Special Effects,' he replies.

'Not bad.'

'Could be worse.'

'Who are you wearing?'

'Olivier Theyskens.'

'Ooh. I'm impressed.'

'I like his hair.'

'You'll love the fit of his clothes.'

'Your clothes fit nicely,' he says, suggestively.

I almost forget I'm sitting there, my mouth gaping open, when Sasha says, 'Susanna? You know Toby Richmond, don't you?'

Leaping to my feet, I say, 'Of course!'

I throw my shoulders back and strut forward, prepared to tell Toby how much I hated him in his last movie. Given that there's no room on his lap, I'll take the seat next to him and shoot the breeze about showbiz.

'Is it true you were in the make-up trailer for two hours every morning just getting the scar right?' I'll ask.

Then I'll toss in a question about the famed 'gift bag' for award presenters on Oscar night. Last year's was worth more than a hundred thousand dollars! They all got Tahitian pearl necklaces! How does Toby feel about the IRS now charging taxes on the former 'freebies'? My hair bounces playfully as I cross the carpet to Toby's leather chair. I grin and hold my hand out to shake his. It hangs there, limp, until Sasha shoves something in it.

'Switch my seat, would you?' she says. 'Next to Toby.'

I look down. A plane ticket lies in my open palm like a piece of toilet paper stuck to the bottom of a shoe. All I can do is blink. It doesn't compute. Toby, clearly a gentleman, reaches his hand around Sasha's tiny waist. I smile, relieved. At least, *he's* going to treat me like a person and shake my hand.

'Make sure I'm on the aisle,' he says, handing me his plane ticket, too.

Toby Richmond returns to nuzzling Sasha's neck. They instantly forget I exist, even though I'm standing there, like a dope, holding their tickets.

'You were awful in *The Man in the Window*,' I mumble, grasping for some dignity. 'In a good way.'

Toby Richmond says, 'Thanks,' then dismisses me with a wave of his hand.

What made me think six months would make any difference? Toby treats me just like Sasha does – a high-school slave. Invisible, until they need me.

Sighing, I lumber out to the front desk of the Admiral's Club to see if I can change two plane tickets.

'Why the glum face?' the woman behind the ticket counter asks me.

'I'm—' I stop and re-evaluate my plight. 'I'm going to the Academy Awards!'

Why let anything bum me out? I, Susanna Barringer, am the luckiest girl in the world!

FOUR

Nell is the first passenger to board the plane. Sasha and Toby join Keith and me as we organise our carry-on luggage. Just as I'm about to ask why we're not boarding, too, the explanation blares over the loudspeaker.

'Business Class passengers, please.'

Ah. I get it. I'm not flying First Class after all. Apparently, First Class is reserved for Queen Nell. Which is okay with me. I'd rather fly Business Class next to Keith, than First Class next to Nell or anyone else.

Keith takes the camera bags from me and hands me my boarding pass. Then I follow him to the gate.

'You're in Group Four,' he says.

'Group Four?'

'Wait until you hear them call your group.'

Bewildered, I watch Keith and the *Scene* team disappear without me. Then I wait. Right into economy. Through Groups One, Two and Three. By the time they call Group Four, most of the passengers have already boarded the

31

plane. I roll my suitcase down the corridor and try not to look crushed.

'All the way to the back,' the flight attendant says as she looks at my boarding pass.

Biting the inside of my lip, I roll through the First Class cabin, where Nell is sipping champagne. She's next to a handsome man with silver hair and a dark tan. Her legs are tucked flirtatiously beneath her. As I pass, she doesn't even look my way. In Business Class, Keith is sitting alone. He's sipping orange juice. When I pass by him, he winks. It looks incredibly cheesy. The least he could have done is tell me I'm flying with the riff-raff so I wouldn't look like such a moron.

'Thanks, Susan,' Sasha mouths to me as I pass her and Toby. They are covered in an airline blanket doing God knows what.

My suitcase bumps against the seats as the aisle narrows in the economy cabin. Checking row numbers, I continue to the back of the plane. The closer I get, the more nauseous I feel. No, please God, no, I silently pray as the pool of potential seat-mates evaporates into a few stragglers at the back. But the Cosmos is hellbent on testing me.

A young mother is sitting in a middle seat. Her baby – yes, her *crying* baby – is strapped to her lap. By the smell of it, he could use a diaper change.

'Is this your row?' she asks.

One last time, I check my ticket. Then, desperate, I look around for another empty seat. But the plane is packed.

'Sorry,' a flight attendant says to me, patting my shoulder as she squeezes past.

'Yes, this is my row,' I finally say.

With no other choice, I stow my luggage in the overhead compartment and sink into my seat.

'He'll quiet down as soon as I change his diaper,' the mom says, lifting her (now wailing) baby onto her lap. 'Would you mind holding the wipes?'

FIVE

My knees are sore from pressing up against the seat in front of me, my lower back is killing me. I have a headache and my tongue feels like it's wearing a sweater. Plus, I already saw the movie, breakfast was a rubbery half-moon they call an omelette, and the mother next to me was right – her baby did quiet down with a fresh diaper. Until he pooped again. Somewhere over Chicago.

Still, as the tyres screech onto the runway at LAX – Los Angeles Airport – my skin tingles with excitement. I'm *here*. Celebrity Central. Tinsel Town. I've even forgiven Keith for not telling me I was seated in the nursery. How can I be blue? Soon I'll be in Hollywood – where the streets are paved with red carpets!

Los Angeles is technically a city unto itself, but people say 'LA' to define a whole chunk of land north of San Diego and south of San Francisco. It's everything from the *boyz* of South Central to the fake boobs of Beverly Hills to the surfers at Malibu. And, of course, Los Angeles is Hollywood. Where Jake G will be waiting for me to deliver Amelia's kiss.

The Los Angeles I'm experiencing at this moment is one massive tangle of freeways. Which are laughably named, because the only thing that's 'free' about this *twelve-lane* highway is the fact that you don't have to pay to sit in traffic. Everything is *brown*. The pavement, the dry hills, the air. I smell exhaust, feel the hot sun burn through the tinted windows. Where are the palm trees? Where is the blue sky?

Oh well. Why look outside when it's so lovely in our limo? I'm sitting next to Keith, across from Nell and Sasha, in the air-conditioned limousine that will be our transportation for the next three days. There's a full bar, a snack-filled fridge, and a plasma TV with a wide selection of DVDs. Through the smoked-glass windows, I can see that everyone we pass is wondering who we are. I know it's true because we inch past another limo and I'm *dying* to know who's hidden behind their windows.

'Martini, anyone?' Nell asks.

Keith and Sasha just grunt.

'Susie?' Nell looks at me.

'Oh, no thanks. I'm too yo—'

'I'm not asking if you *want* one; I'm telling you to make me one.'

'Oh.' A martini is the drink with the olive, right?

Keith comes to my rescue. 'Vodka or gin, Nell?'

Nell glances at her watch. 'What's the local time?'

'Ten-thirty in the morning,' Keith replies.

'Gin, then.'

Martini in hand, Nell leans back against the leather seat and sighs happily. I lean back, too, and reread the schedule Carmen e-mailed me. My heart flutters. The next three days are going to be the best three days of my life.

Oscar Itinerary

SATURDAY: Pre-Oscar Day

Arrive LA.

Limo to Renaissance Hotel in Hollywood. Check in.

Register in press room at Kodak (Oscar) Theatre.

(Note: press room is *in* Renaissance Hotel,
   connected to Kodak Theatre.)

Work with Keith/Nell.

Dinner at hotel.

SUNDAY: Oscar Day

Press room by 1.00.
Red carpet arrivals begin at 3.00.
Show starts at 5.00.
First award presented by 5.30.
Dinner in press room (sandwiches, etc.).
Show scheduled to end by 8.00.
After-parties.

MONDAY: Post-Oscar Day

Hotel check-out.
Return to NYC noon flight.

The best part of my itinerary? (Besides, of course, the red carpet arrivals, kissing Jake G – ha, ha – and seeing Randall Sanders again.) I see lots of openings for me to sneak out and snag my scoop. Forget about New York. If I can make it *here*, I can make it anywhere.

'How much longer, driver?' Nell yells to the front.

The driver – an ageing surfer-type – calls back, 'About twenty minutes.'

'Brilliant. As soon as we get to our hotel in Venice,' Nell says, 'we'll revise the schedule. I need a nap.'

'Venice?!' I whip my head in her direction. 'Venice *Beach*?'

Sasha grunts and says, 'Yes, Venice Beach. The only town that's farther away from Hollywood is Fresno.'

'Carmen told me we were staying at the hotel right next to the Oscar theatre,' I say.

Nell replies, 'Change of plans. Why would I fly three thousand miles into warm weather and not stay at the beach?'

'Three days in traffic,' Keith says, glumly.

'My clothes will be as wrinkled as Joan Rivers' pre-lifted face,' Sasha adds.

Nell tosses the last of her martini down her throat.

'It's all arranged,' she says. 'We'll have our morning staff meeting in the limo on the way to Hollywood. Drinks on the way home to the beach. Brilliant!'

For the first time ever, I want to throw my arms around Nell Wickham's expensively creamed neck. Venice! I know all about Venice Beach. The Boardwalk. Muscle Beach. In-line skaters. White sand, yellow sun, blue surf. In winter!

'How cool is it that we're staying at the beach?' I chirp.

'Kiss arse,' Sasha mumbles under her breath.

'Thank you, Susie,' Nell says. 'Now, be a love and make me another martini.'

SIX

The limo driver exits the freeway and continues straight to the glistening Pacific Ocean. *Now* I see blue sky! Nell drank her second martini in three gulps. Then she offered me a Diet Coke. Which I totally regret accepting. The mixture of excitement, nerves, Keith's dimples, and serious carbonation launched a major burp-fest in my body.

'This is awesome,' I say, as we pass the sign that announces we've entered the city of Venice, population thirty-nine thousand, three hundred and fifty-four.

Burp. 'Excuse me.'

A girl with a henna tattoo walks a dog wearing a red bandana. A guy with a long, grey ponytail wears a T-shirt tie-dyed in a peace sign.

'Didn't anyone tell these people the sixties are over?' Sasha asks, sneering.

The small houses are squished together. Even along the Venice Canal, a lot of the funky old houses look like weeds sprouted from the Earth.

41

'We should do a fashion shoot here some day,' Nell says. 'Real Italian designers on the streets of fake Venice.'

'Brilliant!' I say to Nell.

Both Sasha and Keith roll their eyes.

The driver turns down a narrow alley and parks in front of a closed garage door.

'We're here,' he says.

'Where?' I ask. I smell the ocean, but don't see anything but a string of closed garage doors.

'Check us in, Sue,' Nell says, a bit slurry. 'We're going to dip our toes in the Pacific.'

'No prob,' I reply. Then I gulp. I've been in a hotel only once before. A Holiday Inn Express. While my dad checked us in, Mom and I ate the warm chocolate chip cookies they served in the breakfast room.

'And walk Stella.'

Nell reaches down and pulls a black leather bag up from the floor. Stella pokes her head out of the bag and barks.

'Stella!'

I'm shocked. Nell's *dog* has been with us the whole time?

'Make sure all my clothes are hung on padded hangers,' Nell yells over her shoulder. Then she disappears with Keith and Sasha down a sandy path between two garages.

'That woman is a piece of work.'

Through the window, I see that the limo driver is standing there, stretching his arms over his head. I laugh.

'You noticed?' I ask, stepping out of the car.

'I'm Ted,' he says, extending his hand.

'Susanna,' I reply, reaching around Stella's doggie bag to shake it. Then, letting Nell's cream puff of a dog out of her carrying case, I add, 'This is Stella.'

Stella instantly poops behind the limo's back tyre.

'I have a feeling these three days are going to be the longest month of our lives,' Ted says.

We both laugh. The sun feels good on my face. I'd better apply sunscreen fast. It's warm, not hot, here at the beach. I taste the salt in the air, and hear the faint sound of waves lapping against the shoreline a few yards down the sandy pathway. Barefoot, a surfer passes us on the way to the ocean, his surfboard under one arm and a long zipper dangling from the back of his wetsuit.

Ted's hair is bleached blond. His fingernails are pink ovals and the crinkles around his eyes show how much he loves the sun. I wonder, is every guy in LA a surfer or a surfer wannabe? Ted pops open the trunk and starts pulling suitcases out. The trunk is so huge, it's nearly the size of a New York City studio apartment.

'Since we're in this together,' I say, 'may I ask you a question?'

'Sure.'

'How do you check into a hotel?'

Ted belly-laughs.

'Tell them Nell Wickham is here and stand back.'

Really, it's more of a *house* than a *hotel*. Only two floors high, the exterior is covered in ivy. Hot pink flowers explode everywhere. The grass is so green it looks fake. Stella is having a sniff-fest all over the lawn. Grabbing her, I walk down a red brick pathway, across a huge, shaded porch with white wicker chairs, and through the front door.

'May I help you?'

A man about my dad's age sits behind a large wooden desk. The 'lobby' of this 'hotel' looks just like a living room.

'Nell Wickham is here,' I say.

Ted is right. Dad-Man grabs a walkie-talkie and summons a guy named Jake.

'Stat,' he says, like he's a doctor in the emergency room.

Jake – blond, tan, muscled and surferish (of course!) – comes bounding down the stairs.

'Ms Wickham and her staff are here,' Dad-Man says. 'Please get their bags.'

Surfer Boy jogs off, and Dad-Man looks at me.

'I'm Richard,' he says. 'Welcome. Would you like to see the suites?'

'We're checked in?' I ask.

'All set,' he says.

My face lights up. Who needs Carmen if check-in is this easy and I'm booked into a suite? Hey, I'll even have time to dip my toe in the Pacific, too!

With Stella tucked under my arm, I follow Richard into Keith's suite first. It's on the ground floor, with a view of the garden, a king-sized bed, and a gargantuan shower built for two. I can't help but imagine myself in that bathroom. With candles. And flowers. And, of course, a soapy *Scene* magazine photog scrubbing my back.

Interrupting my fantasy world, Richard leads me upstairs to Nell's suite. It's *gorgeous*. Dark wood floors shine in the sunlight. You can see the Pacific Ocean through the paned windows on either side of the fireplace. And there's a separate room with a striped white and blue couch and matching chair. I can't wait to see my suite!

As if she knows that this is her room, too, Stella wriggles out of my arms and leaps onto the fluffy comforter of Nell's king-sized bed. In a circular snail's shell move, she curls up on one of Nell's pillows. Leaving her there, Richard and I continue the tour.

Sasha's suite, at the back of the house, has its own

entrance. It's white and pretty and feels like a treehouse. This place is *so* much nicer than a Holiday Inn Express!

Richard leads me down a hallway. I notice that each room has its own name. Nell is in the Venice Pier Suite; Keith is in the Olympic Suite. Who cares that I flew in coach this morning? Two nights and three days in my own luxury suite will eradicate the diaper poop that's been filling up my life of late.

'Here's your room,' Richard says.

Room?

I glance at the name on the door: Tramp's Quarters. My smile fades a bit. But I recover quickly. So there's no 'suite' in the name. Who needs a suite when I'm a tiptoe from the ocean?

The door swings open and I step in.

'This is one of our more modest rooms,' Richard says.

He's not kidding. The limousine's trunk feels bigger. For a second, my spirits sag. Then I think, 'Who cares? I don't need a big room! All I need is a bed and a bathroom.'

'Your bathroom is down the hall,' he adds.

'Down the hall?'

Another cosmic joke?

My gaze darts right and left. Unless that tiny closet in the corner is a bathroom, the joke is on me.

'We provide a robe,' Richard offers, helpfully.

46

Suddenly, I hear noises downstairs and Queen Nell's commands.

'We leave in five minutes, people! Susan, make sure Stella gets a bowl of bottled water!'

Richard takes off for the sound of Nell's voice. My impulse is to take off, too. For the beach. Or Venice Boardwalk. Or I can just lock myself in the Tramp's Quarters and hide in the closet that's not a bathroom.

I take a deep breath. Blow it out hard.

'This is no time to be a baby,' I say out loud.

Not when Nell's clothes need to be hung on padded hangers, her dog needs bottled water, and Hollywood is a long, wrinkling limo ride away.

SEVEN

I'm pinching myself. We're here at last. The limo turns left on La Brea, drives past the tar pits, up a hill, around a corner and *poof*! My heart jumps. Above me, tucked into a scruffy foothill, is the famous 'Hollywood' sign. It's smaller than I imagined it. Which is what everyone says about the Statue of Liberty. Clearly, your mind's eye sees things bigger and better than they are. But right now, staring up at the nine free-standing letters, which are a tad crooked, more ivory than pure white, more matt than shiny, I've never seen a more thrilling sight.

The 'staff meeting' in the limo on the way to Hollywood consisted of six sentences and one scoff.

Nell: Susie, keep your mobile on at all times in case I need you.

Me: Okay.

Keith: Nothing much happens until tomorrow.

Me: Ah.

Sasha: I hope that's not what you're planning to wear tomorrow night.

Me: No. I brought a dress.

Sasha (scoffing): A dress?

The eighth sentence was Nell asking for her third martini.

A crowd has already gathered across from the Kodak Theatre, where the stars will shine tomorrow night. They can't get close to the action – the street is blocked off by police barricades. The only traffic allowed are limousines with special permits. Like us.

'Here.' Keith hands me a press pass dangling on a lanyard. 'You lose it, you might as well go home.'

Carefully, I place the lanyard around my neck. I feel the laminated pass settle on my fluttering stomach. A *press* pass. To the Academy Awards. If I couldn't feel the rush of blood racing through my veins, I would swear I was dreaming.

'Keith—' My eyes suddenly blur with tears. I bite my lower lip, search for the right words to express how incredibly grateful I am to be here – in Hollywood – where Randall Sanders will smile and wave at the cheering crowd tomorrow. Where Halle will make jaws drop with her dress and Jamie will be a total fox. As I open my mouth to speak, Keith leaps out of the limo and circles around to the trunk, where he stowed the camera equipment he hired me to carry.

'Leave your stuff in the trunk,' he says to me. 'There's no place to stash it inside.'

I nod. Ted, the limo driver, kills the engine. Sasha hops out, too. And Nell, a bit tipsy, heaves herself up with the help of the door handle.

'Get a grip, Susanna,' I tell myself, sniffing. Bursting into tears before you've even set foot in Hollywood?! That's what a high-school kid would do, not a valued member of the *Scene* team! Taking a deep breath, I run my fingers under my lower lashes. I reach into my pack for gloss and a comb. Then, poking one foot out of the limousine, holding my head high, I rise up into my destiny.

'Crud, she's a nobody!' I hear a disappointed voice moan from the crowd.

'That's what you think,' I reply, my chin jutting forward.

Even though the awards show isn't until tomorrow evening, bleachers are already set up beside the towering golden archway that leads into the glamorous theatre. Workmen in faded blue jeans hook up velvet ropes. A giant golden Oscar dangles from a crane while workmen in hard hats guide it into place next to the majestic doorway. And, yes, there is a red carpet. A cranberry-red carpet lining the sidewalk and walkway leading up to the theatre. I swear it glows in the bright sunlight. Like it's been sprinkled with shimmering stardust.

Nell and Sasha are already inside. Everyone but Nell wears a press pass.

'The only things I wear around my neck are diamonds or pearls,' she said, tossing her pass in the back seat of the limo.

As he did at the airport, Keith drapes two camera bags across my shoulders. He then grabs the remaining bag and slings it across his own. Impossibly, in the unforgiving white sunlight of LA, after a six-hour flight, no sleep the night before, no shave this morning, Keith Franklin looks better than ever.

'As soon as you need me, call,' Ted says, handing us business cards with his cell number on it. 'I'll be five minutes away.'

Ted slams the trunk shut as Keith and I make our way across the red carpet to the gorgeous Kodak Theatre. My whole body is electrified with excitement.

'*Scene* magazine.' I flash my press pass at the police officer guarding the security checkpoint. He nods and waves me through a metal detector.

Oh, no. That morning at the airport, the metal in my

underwire bra set off the security alarm. Much to Keith's amusement, the female guard totally felt me up. Now will we have Round Two? Why, oh why, did I let the saleswoman at Victoria's Secret convince me that the 'architecture' of Infinity Edge would give me the 'womanly' lift I so 'desperately' need? Sasha is a fashion diva and she's totally flat!

'Don't worry,' Keith says. 'They set the sensitivity low. Do you have any idea how much metal is in a designer gown? They'd be beeping all night.'

He's right. I sail through security. Nothing can stop me now.

Together, Keith and I walk across the most famous red carpet in the world. I still can't believe I'm here – allowed into the 'off-limits' area. I'm walking where Drew will pose. Where Denzel will wave. Will Maggie G and Jake G arrive together? I'm on the *inside*. I can't stop smiling. The camera bags are criss-crossed over my pounding heart. The hottest celebrity photographer in New York is ahead of me. Nell Wickham is inside the theatre, waiting for my teenage take on the big event.

Can life get any better?

As I sashay under the polished archway, I wink at the humungous golden Oscar, now in place. Just like that, I'm *in*.

'Sheesh!' I say out loud.

The interior of the building is awesome. A wide, red staircase leads up to the main theatre lobby. The carpet feels soft beneath my sneakers. The air-conditioning is a cool *kiss-kiss* on each cheek. I'm walking in the footsteps of Nicole, Uma, Hilary. I can almost feel the train of my satin gown trailing behind me. The cheer of the crowd washes over me in a glorious echo.

Susanna-na-na! We love you-ou-ou!

My public. They love me; they really love me. I feel invincible. I'm in the centre of the celebrity universe. Its power is tangible. There's no stopping me now. My desti—

'Susie,' Nell shouts from the top of the stairs, 'stop dawdling and find me the VIP loo. I've forgotten where it is.'

It's clear that Hollywood's Kodak Theatre was *built* for the Academy Awards. Regular stuff, like plays and concerts, happen all year round, but tomorrow night – Oscar night – is their reason for being. And it shows. Massive photographs of past and present Oscar-winners like Grace Kelly, Jack Nicholson and Julia Roberts line the walls of the *five* lobbies that rise straight up in the air. A sweeping staircase spirals up the middle like a soft tornado lifting stars into heaven.

Keith takes the two camera bags off my shoulders and I hurry up the stairs, looking for a place for Nell to pee.

'Is the VIP restroom up here?' I ask a security officer on the second floor.

He takes one look at my press pass and says, 'Not for you.'

Stunned, I cop an attitude. 'It's not *for* me. It's for Nell Wickham.' Then, cocking one eyebrow in a superior way, I add, 'The editor-in-chief of *Scene* magazine.'

He stiffens. 'Definitely *not* Nell Wickham.'

Now, I'm speechless. Nell Wickham refused entrance into a bathroom? Did the officer hate the last issue of *Scene*? Was he offered money to squeal on a celeb? Was it not enough? Did he think we were unfair in our coverage of Celebrity Politicians. Did he actually vote for Arnold??

'This is the bathroom for the *stars*,' he explains. 'No press allowed.'

I roll my eyes. 'Can't we all go together?'

'You're new to this business,' he says, smiling patiently.

'Well, not *new* per se, bu—'

'If we let the press in there,' he interrupts, 'they'll plant a microphone or a toilet cam. Can you imagine the conversations between Oscar nominees while they stand at the mirror? Not to mention the embarrassing photos that would be plastered all over the Internet.'

'There's a toilet cam?' I ask.

'There is *every* kind of camera. Tell your boss she can use the facilities where every other reporter does. In the press room.'

'Where's the press room?'

He points. 'At the end of the Winner's Walk.'

Okay. I admit it. I can't help myself. I know Nell's bladder is ready to release its martinis, but how can I pass up a chance to see the Academy Award Winner's Walk? Nell didn't *say* it was an emergency. In fact, I remember once camping with my parents in the Adirondacks and holding it all night because I swear I heard a growl over by the outhouse. I'm living proof that you don't always have to answer instantly when nature calls.

A two-minute detour? What's the big whoop? I'll just tell her I was making sure the loo was good enough for her British bum. Or something more refined, like needing to sweep the room for hidden toilet cams.

The Winner's Walk is a wide hallway behind a floor-to-ceiling glass wall. One end of the 'walk' is backstage where the awards will be presented tomorrow night; the other end is the press room. Clearly, this is where the stars pass through – clutching Oscar – after they've given their

56

acceptance speeches. Right now, the air smells of Windex, and two guys in cargo shorts cart in small, high tables with big mirrors. The mirrors are framed in round light bulbs. The workmen disappear through a side door, and return carrying director's chairs. I watch as they pop the director's chairs open and set them in front of the mirrors.

'Check the curtain pulley,' one of the guys yells to the other.

Just like that, a red velvet drape closes across my side of the glass wall. The Winner's Walk disappears from view. Until, of course, I lift the curtain and sneak under it.

'Hair and make-up?' the worker asks through the glass.

Shaking my head no, I say, 'Press,' even though I'm nervous after the bathroom rejection. Will he think I'm here to plant a Winner's Walk cam?

He doesn't ask me to leave, which I take as an invitation to stay and watch. Hopefully, Nell can hold it a wee bit longer.

'What's happening in here?' I ask, stepping closer, nearly pressing my nose to the glass.

'We're setting up the "Tears and Repairs" room,' he says.

'Tears and what?'

He flags me over to the side. I nearly faint when he

opens a door in the glass wall and says, 'Come on in.'

In. It's my favourite word in the English language. That, plus 'zaftig' and 'swain', which really mean 'chubby' and 'boyfriend' but sound much better. *In* means *access.* It means 'not out'. *In* means that I, Susanna Barringer, am one step closer to dazzling Nell Wickham with my uncanny ability to ferret out a great story, to boldly go (or go boldly, if I want to ignore *Star Trek* and be grammatically correct) where no reporter has gone before, to prove that I'm no mere high-school inter—

'Are you going to just stand there?'

I walk through the door. Just like that I'm in.

'A virgin?'

My chest clutches. Is it that obvious?

'Your first time at the Academy Awards?' he clarifies.

Exhaling, I say, 'Yeah.' He then says, 'We call this the "Tears and Repairs" room. Tomorrow night, the biggest stars in the world will come out, grabbing their little gold man, crying like newborns. This hallway – the Winner's Walk – is where a team of make-up artists will blow their noses and dab their tears and repair all the make-up that's running down their faces.'

'Seriously?'

'Seriously. Even the guys need some cover-up before they face photographers from every corner of the globe.

You'd be amazed how many of them burst into tears the moment they step off that stage.'

My heart lurches. Oliver Stone weeping like a girl? Now *that's* a scoop.

'Plus the flop sweat is phenomenal. We're talking Niagara Falls.'

'Hey,' I say casually. 'Do you think I could pop by tomorrow night and hang out for a few minutes?'

'Hang out?' he says. 'In here? Inside the Winner's Walk?'

'Yeah,' I repeat. 'Just for a few minutes. I'll hide behind the curtains.'

'Hide behind the curtains, you say?'

'I won't move. I promise. Look.' Taking tiny breaths, like a panting kitten, I show the worker how my belly only flutters. 'No one will know I'm here.'

He stares at me a moment then says, 'Why not?'

My jaw drops. 'You'll let me in tomorrow night?'

'Of course,' he says. 'Why wouldn't I let a reporter hide behind the curtains and watch stars cry? Hey, I know! Why don't you bring your camera? That way, you can get a great shot of an actor looking *awful*. Like, maybe Nicole Kidman will have black mascara streaming down her face. Or Adrien Brody will have a runny nose. Stars love candid shots like that! And me, well, I love pumping gas. Which works out perfectly, because that's what I'll be doing right after I'm fired.'

I make a face. He pats my shoulder.

'Tomorrow night, this curtain will be closed and guarded. This door will be locked. You will be where you belong – in the press room with everyone else.'

With that, he guides me to the door and ushers me *out* the same way he ushered me in.

'Nice try, though,' he adds, smiling.

I smile, too. He doesn't know what I know: I'm a native New Yorker. I'm *wily*. Somewhere, there is an awesome scoop that no other celebrity reporter will be able to get. Somehow, I'm going to be the girl who finds it.

EIGHT

By the time I'm back down the spiral staircase, Nell is gone. Keith and Sasha are gone, too. A zap of panic shoots through my body. Will Keith be mad about my detour into the 'Tears and Repairs' room? He did, after all, fly me to Hollywood to help *him*.

As if on cue, my cell rings. It's Keith.

'I'm on my way,' I say into the phone.

'Where?' he asks.

'Wherever you are. Where, by the way, are you?'

Keith laughs. 'I'm in the press room,' he says, 'but I need you to run back to the limo.'

'The limo? Why?'

'They won't let Nell in without her press pass.'

Now I laugh. 'Really?'

'It's ridiculous, but security is super tight and they are going by the book.'

'No problem, Keith,' I say. 'I'll meet you in the press room – with Nell's pass – in ten minutes.'

Keith hangs up as I pull Ted's business card out of my back pocket and dial his cell.

'Nell has a wardrobe malfunction,' I say.

Ted laughs when I tell him what's going on.

'Meet me where I dropped you off,' he says. 'I'll be there in five minutes.'

Admittedly, it's not very classy. But I can't help feeling a little smug about Nell's comeuppance. Which is another one of my favourite words. It's gratifying to watch the Universe swat you down when you get too high and mighty. It's taken Nell a long time to get hers. Though it's tacky of me, I'm glad I'm here to witness it. Nell Wickham is being treated just like everyone else. Hollywood really is the land of magic!

By the time I make my way down the entrance staircase and through the golden archway, Ted is exactly where he said he would be.

'The whole street is blocked off. How did you get here so fast?' I ask.

He smiles devilishly. 'Limo driver's secret passageway.'

Ted opens the passenger door of the limo, and we both climb in to look for Nell's pass. The air-conditioning feels cool on my face.

Ted asks me, 'How long – on average – do you think it takes to drive a star to the Academy Awards?'

Sitting still for a moment, I rest my chin on my hand. I'd been in Los Angeles less than a day and already I'd spent most of it in traffic. Oscar 'night' actually begins at about five in the afternoon. The red carpet parade starts two hours before that. Since Hollywood is in the middle of Los Angeles, and most stars live in Beverly Hills or Bel-Air or Malibu or one of the canyons, they are at least forty-five minutes away. To be safe, they'd have to allow an hour and a half for traffic. Mentally running the figures, I finally say, 'Two hours. On average.'

He grins. 'Try five minutes.'

'Yeah, right,' I say.

'I'll let you in on a little secret, Susanna. The presenters and nominees all spend tonight in the hotel that's attached to the Kodak Theatre. Tomorrow, when you see the limos driving up and dropping off the stars, take a close look at the *drivers*. It's the same guys over and over. They just circle the block, picking up and dropping off. It rarely takes more than a few minutes.'

My jaw drops.

'The *Renaissance* Hotel?'

'Yep.'

'The hotel where we were originally staying?'

'The very place.'

I groan. Who cares about the stupid Pacific Ocean when Josh Hartnett was just down the hall?!

'How do you know this?' I ask Ted.

'Peek into the drivers' seats tomorrow night. One of them will be me.'

'No way,' I say, agog.

'Since the Queen and her court don't need me until the show is over, I'm picking up a few extra bucks.'

'That is so cool,' I say.

'Driving a limo on Oscar night is like a box of chocolates,' Ted says, imitating Forrest Gump. 'You never know who you're going to get.'

NINE

My mind is racing. So are my feet. With Nell's press pass lanyard flapping in my hands, I flash my own pass, dash through the metal detector and race up the staircase to the press room.

'Here,' I gasp, 'it is.'

Nell snatches the pass and practically shoves it up the security officer's nose.

'Satisfied?' she asks, snottily.

'Thank you, ma'am,' he says, stone-faced. Then he moves away from the door and lets us both enter.

I've never seen so many cameras in my life. There are tripods, cords, lights and gigantic lenses all squished in front of a makeshift stage. I hear Japanese, German, Spanish, French and a couple of languages I can't even recognise. The press room – normally a big conference room – is actually part of the hotel. But it's attached to the Kodak Theatre for easy access. Tomorrow night, the stars will get their hair and make-up repaired in the

Winner's Walk, then they'll pass through a door and swim into a sea of reporters from all over the world. Keith told me they all come a day early to stake out their positions, sweet-talk publicists, and pray they never sold an unflattering shot of a potential Oscar winner to the tabloids. If they did, they pray the publicist doesn't recognise them. As I look around, I see more than a few photographers in dark glasses.

'Keith!' I spot him by one of the huge coffee urns. Keith, of course, is chatting with a beautiful woman in a very tight T-shirt.

'I need to talk to you,' I blurt out, my own chest still heaving.

'This is my assistant, Susanna,' he says, introducing me. 'Susanna, meet Helene. She's covering the awards for the French newspaper, *Le Figaro*.'

I nod, trying not to feel jealous. Helene's hair is straight and shiny. No one would ever call her 'Mop Top' (thanks, Sasha!) if she once made the mistake of using a brush on a humid day instead of a comb.

'I'm sorry to interrupt,' I say, 'but can I talk to you for a moment?'

Keith sighs. Helene says, 'Meet me for a drink later?'

Of course, he says yes. Actually, he says, 'Mais oui,' which, of course, would sound totally smarmy if it came out of anyone else's mouth. *My* mouth is hanging open. Keith has a *date* before Nell's even made it to the loo?

'What?' Keith asks me, as I pull him over to a quiet corner.

'They're here,' I whisper.

'Who's where?'

'The stars. They're all here. In the hotel. Tonight.'

'Yeah. So?'

I blink.

'So shouldn't we sneak in and get some photos?'

Keith bursts out laughing. 'Gee, Susanna! I wonder if anyone has ever thought of that before?'

I blink again.

'Look,' he says, 'I admire your spunk, but security is tighter in this hotel than it is at the White House.'

'You knew they would all be in there?' I ask. 'Hilary, Owen, Keira, all of them?'

Keith wraps his arms around my shoulder. '*We* know they are there, and *they* know we are here. That's how the game is played.'

'So all you do is stand here and wait for tomorrow night and take the same pictures everyone else takes?'

'Got any better ideas?'

This time I *don't* blink. I hang my shoulders on a hanger, hold my head up and say, 'As a matter of fact, I do.'

Keith raises both luscious eyebrows. 'Like what?'

'Like ... like ... like I have no idea.' My shoulders sag.

'Look, Susanna, tomorrow is the big show. You'll be standing in this room, with me, doing whatever I ask you to do. We're going to get great shots of the clothes, the hair, the shoes – all the stuff everyone wants to see. That's why we're here.'

'There's got to be more,' I say. 'With every star in the Universe under our noses, there has to be a *scoop*.'

He grins. His dimples are almost unbearable.

'I'm sure all kinds of scoops are brewing. But our job is to take fabulous photos tomorrow night.'

'And until then?' I ask, my eyes wide.

Keith shakes his head, smiles again.

'I'll tell you what, Susanna,' he says. 'I don't need you full-time until the show starts tomorrow after five. If I do, I'll call your cell. But right now, give it a shot. Unless Nell needs you, you have about twenty-four hours to get your scoop.'

My eyes light up. 'You mean it?'

'I'll work it out with Nell.'

'You're the best,' I say, nearly bursting.

'Don't do anything illegal, grossly immoral or embar-rassing to the magazine. Other than that, go for it.'

68

Before I even realise what I'm doing, I throw my arms around Keith's neck and kiss his stubbly cheek.

'Thank you,' I say.

'Don't thank me. I'm not doing anything other than getting out of your way.'

'That's all I need,' I sing.

Turning on my heels, I head for the exit with my press pass around my neck and absolutely no clue what to do next.

TEN

The second-floor lobby is a beehive of activity. Reporters stream into the press room, a florist sets a giant vase of white flowers on a pedestal in front of the Winner's Walk, a guy in a uniform waxes the railing of the giant spiral staircase. I take it all in, plotting my strategy. Perhaps I'll interview the man with the vacuum cleaner? Does he also vacuum the hallways of the hotel next door? Or, better yet, I'll—

'May I help you?'

Whipping my head around, I'm nose-to-nose with a security officer.

'I'm press,' I say, proudly holding up my pass.

He laughs. 'Your school paper sent you to the Academy Awards?'

'*Scene* magazine,' I reply, superiority creeping into my voice. 'Special teen assignment.'

'I see,' he says, looking like he doesn't believe me. 'Well, whatever assignment you're on, if you have a press pass, you go straight to the press room.'

'What?' I gulp.

'No press are allowed to wander around the theatre.'

'But—'

'No exceptions.'

With gentle, but firm, pressure on my back, the guard leads me right back where I came from – the press room door.

'My special teen assign—'

He opens the door. I want to cry. Not even five minutes into my scoop-search and I'm already foiled?

'Have a nice day,' the guard says, making sure I walk through the open door.

So much for my brilliant career.

Humiliated, I don't want Keith to see me. I peek over at the coffee urns. He's not there. He's probably off somewhere with Helene, working on international relations. A quick search of the room doesn't reveal him, either. Maybe he's in the loo?

The press room is a deafening blend of accents. Standing against the wall near the door, I let the foreign words wash over me while I consider my next move. Suddenly, I smell something. *Ham*. Then I realise something critical. I'm starving. Is it really ham, I wonder, or the scent of oversized egos?

Creeping along the edge, I follow my nose. There, like a beautiful mirage, is the food table. Mini sandwiches, melon slices, bags of chips, cookies. Thankfully, I don't see anyone from *Scene*. Nell has probably ordered a low-carb, low-cal, organic meal from a private caterer, and Sasha doesn't eat. If my phone doesn't ring, I'll have time to eat lunch in peace while I develop a Plan B.

The food table is swarming. You'd think the reporters just landed in Hollywood from a deserted island! I can barely wiggle my hand in far enough to grab a sandwich, a plastic cutlery bundle, and a soda. The sandwich turns out to be roast beef, which is yummy. Bound by a rubber band, the cutlery bundle includes a handy napkin. And what I thought was a soda is really bottled water. Which is fortunate, because I can't afford another burpfest. Not when I have serious scooping to do.

In the far corner of the press room, away from the cameras and the food, I find an empty chair and sit down to eat and think.

If you have a press pass, you go straight to the press room.

That phrase runs over and over in my head. I even find myself chewing to the rhythm of the words. *Press pass* (chew, chew), *press room* (chew, chew).

No exceptions.

I sigh. If I can't make something of an opportunity like this, I don't deserve to be a valued member of the *Scene* team.

But how? Think, Susanna, think.

Press pass (chew, chew), *press room* (chew, chew).

Taking a swig of water, I feel its coolness slide down my throat. Then my mouth flies open.

'I've got it!' I say out loud.

No one pays any attention to me. Which is exactly the way I want it.

Snarfing down my sandwich, I leap to my feet. Nobody said I *had* to wear my press pass, did they? If I'm not wearing a press pass, why do I have to stay in the press room? Didn't Keith Franklin teach me that the secret to being a great celebrity photographer is to lie low? Act like you belong? Isn't that what makes a great celeb reporter, too? I'll just blend in with everyone outside the press room until I spot my scoop. Maybe I'll even grab a rag and start dusting!

Brilliant!

Stashing my press pass in the back pocket of my jeans, next to my comb and lipgloss, I grab the rubber band from my cutlery bundle and scoop my hair into a tight ponytail. Later, before I see Keith again, I'll release sexy tendrils. For now, in case I run into the same security guard who escorted me back to the press room, I want to look as unlike myself as I can.

Feeling invincible, I march straight for the exit – my destiny on the other side of the door.

ELEVEN

First stop: upstairs. Wherever my scoop will be, I know it's *not* on the floor crawling with reporters. I, Susanna Barringer, must boldly go where no wannabe reporter would dare to go. To the *top*. Acting like I belong, my press pass pressing against my butt in my back pocket, I quickly climb the stairs. Thank God our elevator is broken so often. By the time I reach the fifth floor, I'm only gasping instead of heaving.

Lobby Five looks similar to the four lobbies I passed on the way up. It's a big, round room surrounding a large, central spiral staircase. But it's quieter on the fifth floor. The cleaning crew have either done up here, or they are working their way up. I'm grateful for a quiet moment to catch my breath and plot my next move.

'Can I help you?'

My head whips around. Once again, I'm nose-to-nose with a security guard. What's the matter with these people? Don't they ever take a break?

'I'm … I'm …' I stutter. My mind races with every possible explanation why a high-school sophomore, a wily New Yorker in a rigid ponytail, a panting kid, is standing against a wall searching for a scoop.

'I'm looking for my mom,' I blurt out.

'Your mom?' the guard asks.

'Yes,' I say, swallowing hard. 'My name is Susanna. Susanna *Streep*.'

'Oh,' he says, scanning me up and down. I can tell he thinks Meryl Streep, my so-called 'mom', got ripped off by Mother Nature.

'I look like my dad,' I mutter. Then, remembering last summer when Keith Franklin totally took on the personality of a crew member on the set of Randall Sanders' show, *Caught Off-Guard* and marched through it like he owned the place, I get all haughty and ask, 'Well? Have you seen my mother?'

Honestly, I can't tell if my heart is hammering in my chest because I'm out of shape or out of my mind. Either way, I'm sure the guard will soon hear it and bust me, so I brazenly walk past him.

'Never mind,' I call over my shoulder. 'I'll find her myself.'

To my astonishment, he doesn't follow me. I have no idea where I'm going, but several sets of double doors along the rim of the round lobby seem to lead into the theatre.

'Please God,' I whisper, 'don't let Meryl Streep be standing on the other side of the door.'

As if I lived there, I fling open the double door and walk into the room I've seen a million times on TV. It's awesome. Rows of plush red seats, a round ceiling that sparkles like a silver tiara, elegant boxes that jut out from the walls like ornate balconies. The inside of the famous Kodak Theatre reminds me of those huge hoop dresses they wore in the South – all pretty and lacy.

Quickly, I move away from the door and circle all the way around to the far end of the theatre – as far from the security guard as possible. Then I plop down. Taking a deep breath, I lean back and close my eyes.

Again, I wait for security to escort me out. But no one comes.

'Wow,' I say to myself. 'It worked. All I had to do was fib?'

My conscience corrects my vocabulary. You mean *lie*, it tells me. But I quickly justify my, uh, *untruth* by labelling it as being undercover. Keith warned me not to do anything *grossly* immoral. Lying about my parentage, I figure, is only truly gross if I'm trying to get an inheritance, right? Pretending to be Meryl Streep's daughter to get into a theatre – well, that's just savvy reporting.

Isn't it?

Before my head starts spinning, I open my eyes. Suddenly, in a series of heavy metallic sounds, the stage lights go on far below me. A man in headphones stands close to the edge of the stage. From where I'm sitting – directly above the farthest corner – he's in profile. He says something into the microphone that curls around his cheek. I see him nod to someone backstage, then as suddenly as the stage lights came on, the floor lights rise up in a rush of brightness. I squint at first, then gasp. There, like gigantic paper dolls, are huge blow-ups of all my favourite actors. Their poster-sized portraits are propped up on the orchestra seats.

'Move Russell Crowe to the aisle,' the guy with the microphone says. 'And make sure Cate is up front.'

On the floor, two young guys in jeans scurry over to the posters and move them as directed.

'That's good,' Microphone Man says, surveying the celebrity seating arrangement for tomorrow night. 'What-ever we do, make sure Uma isn't sitting next to Oprah.'

I hear a chuckle from the stage. Then I hear the faint sound of a door opening and the pad of footsteps coming ever closer.

My stomach drops.

'Miss Streep?' a voice says, tapping my shoulder.

I don't move, trying to melt into the soft seat.

'Will you please come with me?'

'No thanks,' I reply, avoiding eye contact. 'I'll wait here for my mom.'

The voice erupts into a loud guffaw. 'Whoever your mother really is, she's not meeting you here.'

Now I look up.

'Nice try,' the security guard says. The same one I saw on my way in.

Taking me by the arm, he pulls me out of my beautiful plush seat in the gorgeous Kodak Theatre.

'But, I—' I protest.

Clearly, he's not interested. Without a word, he escorts me out the double door, into the lobby, over to the spiral staircase, and down five flights of carpeted stairs. I consider producing my press pass, but something tells me that would get me into bigger trouble.

'How did you bust me?' I finally ask.

'Gummer,' he says.

'Gummer?'

'I looked it up. Meryl Streep is married to Don Gummer. Their children's last names are *Gummer*, not Streep.'

'Oh,' I say sheepishly. Then I ask, 'What's with that anyway? Why should all your kids have your husband's name? I mean, couldn't it be fifty-fifty?'

The guard doesn't answer. What he *does* is accompany me all the way out the front door of the Kodak Theatre, across the gleaming red carpet, past the police barricades. Before I can formulate Plan C, I'm thrust into the riff-raff in the blinding sunlight of Hollywood, California.

'There's that nobody again,' I hear someone say.

At that moment, it feels painfully true.

TWELVE

I'm bummed. And hot. What's up with this state? Don't they know it's winter? My sunscreen is in my backpack in the limo. If I come home with a sunburn, Mom will tan my hide.

Just as I'm snaking through the onlookers for the shade of an awning, I see a limo round the corner. The crowd surges, pushing me back to the barricades.

'Who's in there?' someone shouts. 'Can you see? Can you?'

First, I look to see if Ted is driving. He isn't. Then, swept up in the excitement of the crowd, I stand and watch – breathless – as the limo pulls up in front of the Kodak Theatre. The passenger door opens, a leg pokes out, then another, then the full body of a full-blown star.

'It's Felicity Huffman!' I squeal.

Wearing a baseball cap and dark black shades (of course), Ms Huffman turns to the crowd and waves. Her awesome bod is evident, even though she's dressed in jeans and a small pink T-shirt. She smiles and I'm quite sure I've never seen more stunning teeth.

'She's an hour early!' someone in the crowd says.

I turn around. 'An hour?' I scoff. 'Try a *day*.'

Instantly, I'm put in my place. 'She's here for *rehearsal*, you idiot,' a woman in gigantic glasses clutching an autograph book says. 'Felicity is a presenter. The only desperate housewife ever nominated.'

Oh.

The limo pulls away and Felicity Huffman waves once more before disappearing into the theatre. The same theatre where I was only a few moments ago. On the *inside*. Where rehearsals are about to begin. A true reporter would have known this!

Yes, I'm bummed. I'm down . . . but I'm not out.

'Of course I know she's a presenter,' I say, attempting to recover my pride. 'I'm a reporter. For *Scene* magazine.'

The bespectacled woman erupts in a belly laugh. She flags a friend.

'Lookie here!' she says. 'This kid says she's a reporter for *Scene*.'

The crowd roars with laughter. I gaze at them serenely. Raising one eyebrow in an admittedly stuck-up way, I reach my hand around to my back pocket – then have a heart attack.

It's gone.

My press pass is *gone.* So is my lipgloss and comb.

Suddenly, I can't breathe. Sweat instantly beads on my upper lip. Jamming my hand into my other pocket, I feel nothing but fabric. Frantically, I check every pocket, every fold, every nook and cranny on my being. Nothing but my cell phone and Ted's business card.

I'm doomed.

You lose it. You might as well go home. I hear Keith's voice in my head.

Spinning on my heels, I ask the crowd, 'Has anyone seen my press pass?'

Not even the deafening laughter can drown out the thudding sound of my heart as it hits the pit of my stomach. I can't even retrace my steps to see where the pass may have fallen out. Without a press pass, the police will stop me before I can make it past the barricade.

Hey! Was it stolen? Isn't that a crime?

'Excuse me,' I say to one of the police officers guarding the barricades. 'I'd like to report a theft.'

'A theft?' he asks.

'Yes. I'm Susanna Barringer, a reporter for *Scene* magazine. My press pa—'

'You're a reporter for *Scene* magazine?' he says. 'Didn't I just see you carted out by security?'

'Yes, well, that was a misunderstanding.'

He laughs. I start to explain Plan B. But even I hear the ridiculousness of it the moment I utter the words, 'Susanna Streep'. It soon becomes clear that an officer who is sworn to uphold the law doesn't define 'undercover' quite as loosely as I do. He just sees it as a big, fat lie.

'Please step back, miss,' he says. 'Behind the barricades.'

Comeuppance.

I'm tanked. Who cares about a stupid sunburn? I'm already toast.

Briefly, I think of calling Keith and begging for mercy. But how can I admit to losing my press pass barely an hour after he gave it to me? How can I reward his faith in me by being such a loser?

No – there is *no way* I'm going to tell anyone about this. Not when I'm a wily New Yorker who can figure some way out. Or, more accurately, a way *in*.

'Take a deep breath,' I say to myself. *Think.* All you have to do is figure out how to crash the hottest rehearsal in the world. How hard could it be?

THIRTEEN

'Amelia?'

My voice is mousy as I call my best friend in New York for moral support.

'Susanna! How is it going?'

Looking to my left, I see another limo pull up in front of the Kodak Theatre. The crowd erupts.

'Tom! Tom! Tom!' they shriek.

'Great,' I say into the phone. 'Tom Hanks just arrived.'

'Is he nice? Are you going to interview him?'

'He seems nice,' I say, watching Tom Hanks step out of his limousine and wave to the crowd.

Again, the mob explodes. 'Tom! Tom! You were awesome in *The Da Vinci Code*!'

'Who are all those people?' Mel asks.

'People?' I stall for time.

'Those people shouting all around you.'

'They're . . . they're . . . oh, Mel!' Suddenly, I burst into tears.

'What is it?' Mel asks. 'Is it Tom?'

Blubbering, I say, 'It's Tom, Felicity, Brad, Angelina, Meryl Gummer, and every other celebrity I'm never going to meet!'

With that, I open my mouth and let the whole pathetic story come tumbling out. Right there in the middle of the riff-raff, of which I am now an official member.

'Ooh,' Mel says. 'Ah.'

For the next fifteen minutes, my best friend soothes me with the sounds of commiseration. I stake out a quiet patch of sidewalk, away from the barricades, under an awning, in front of a locksmith.

'So my pass and my gloss and my comb could be *anywhere*,' I moan.

Sniff.

'Yikes,' she says.

'Keith is going to kill me.' *Sniff. Sniff.*

'Ouch.'

'My big chance to impress Nell Wickham down the drain!'

'Okay,' Mel says.

'Okay?' *Sni—*

'Do you have a mirror?' she asks me.

'A mirror?'

'You know,' she says, her tone changed completely,

'a reflection device? One of those shiny silver things you look into make sure you don't have sesame seeds stuck in your teeth?'

'No,' I say. 'My mirror is in my backpack and it's in the limo.'

Amelia sighs. 'Is there a window nearby? Anything that can reproduce your likeness?'

I turn around. There, in the streaked glass of the locksmith window, beneath the neon sign that reads '24-Hour Service', is my face.

'Oh, God,' I say, mourning the loss all over again, 'I really need that comb.'

The rubber band pulls my hair out as I pull *it* out. No need to be incognito now, is there? Without gloss, my lips are two pale earthworms resting beneath my nose. I groan.

'Take a good look at your face, Susanna,' Mel says.

My mascara has pooled into two black mocking smiles beneath my lower lashes. In the neon glow, I see a pimple forming on my chin.

'What is this?' I ask. 'Aversion therapy?'

'Are you looking at your face?' she asks, ignoring me.

'Unfortunately, yes.'

'Straight into your eyes?'

'Yes. What are you tr—'

89

'Tell me one thing, Susanna Barringer,' my best friend says. 'Is this the face of a girl who gives up?'

I blink.

'Is this the face of a girl who takes no for an answer?'

I inhale.

'Is this the fa—?'

'All right! I get it,' I say.

'Good. Now, I'm going to hang up and you're going to turn around and figure out a way back into the Kodak Theatre. Right?'

I sigh.

'Right?' she asks impatiently.

'Right,' I say.

'I didn't hear you.'

'Right!'

The woman with the autograph book looks at me, alarmed. I wipe the mascara away from my eyes and the snot away from my nose. I know something she doesn't know. I, Susanna Barringer, am a wily New Yorker who can do *anything* – even crash the Academy Awards.

'I love you, Mel,' I say into the phone.

'Of course you do,' she says right back at me.

90

FOURTEEN

A back entrance – there must be dozens of them! Or, at least *three* for the sides of the theatre that aren't visible. How hard can it be to sneak through a back door when all eyes are up front? Sniffing my last sniff, I toss my rubber band in the trash, fluff up my curls, tuck my cell *deep* into my *front* pocket and head east on Hollywood Boulevard.

'Lookie, everyone!' the woman in the gargantuan glasses shouts. 'Lois Lane is leaving!'

They all laugh, but I don't care. I'll have the last laugh on everyone.

Proudly, I step on the Walk of Fame stars for Ron Howard, Burt Reynolds and Steve McQueen. As soon as I can, I turn left, back into the blaring sun. I cross Hollywood Boulevard and hug the barricades. Every ten feet or so, an LAPD police officer nods at me as if to say, 'Move along, kid.' I smile, keep moving.

The Kodak Theatre, I quickly discover, is part of a mammoth shopping mall. There are restaurants and stores and a Starbucks. The Hollywood Boulevard entrance is blocked off, of course, but I'm able to blend in with the crowd along a wide passageway leading to a round courtyard full of stores.

Instinctively, I scan for stars. Then I roll my eyes. Get real, Susanna. No celebrity in his or her right mind would venture into this tourist ant colony.

I keep walking, head for the hills, end up on Highland Avenue. From there, I turn left and try to reach the back entrance to the theatre via Orchid. I can *see* doors. I even see a loading dock, but they are blocked off, too. It's *totally* annoying. Growing more desperate by the moment, I swing all the way around the block to Orange Avenue. There, in a wide semicircle, is the Orange Court – an outdoor plaza lined with orange and lemon trees. I scurry around the loop, my eyes on the theatre ahead of me. There's definitely an entrance, but it, too, is heavily guarded by uniformed officers.

'Does the city of Los Angeles know that its police force is huddled around a *theatre*?' I shout. 'Aren't there any crimes in this town?'

Thankfully, no one pays attention to me. It's like the streets of New York. Crazy outbursts are greeted with a shrug and a wide circle around the nutcase. Which is fortunate, because unless Lindsay Lohan drives drunk or

Hugh Grant makes another unbelievably dumb mistake, I'll never get a scoop from jail.

Frustrated, I find myself back on Ron Howard's star, furious at the terrorists who've made even the Academy Awards harder to get into than size six jeans.

There's no other way.

I *have* to do it.

Dread envelops me like a mud slide. I have to call Keith.

But, I tell myself, I don't have to call him this *minute*.

It's a beautiful day. Why not take in the sights of Hollywood's most famous street?

Instead of heading east, I walk west. Past the cement handprints and footprints in front of Grauman's Chinese Theatre, where Marilyn Monroe is next to Sophia Loren, and Warren Beatty is next to Whoopi Goldberg. Across the street is the famous Hollywood Roosevelt Hotel, which is supposed to have a haunted ninth floor. I'm tempted to check it out for myself, but the sun feels good and I'd rather spot a live celeb than a dead one. Even though it would be cool to ask Marilyn what *really* happened on the last day of her life.

As I cross the street, I'm stunned to see cars actually stop for me. No, I'm definitely not in New York City any more!

Bette Midler, Bill Cosby, Aretha Franklin, Tom Cruise

and even Snow White have stars on Hollywood Boulevard. I walk over all of them as I circle back to the Kodak Theatre. An actor dressed like Frankenstein's monster tries to lure me into the Wax Museum. Frankly, I'm more interested in the 'freak' museums: Ripley's Believe It or Not and The Guinness World Records. Both sit side-by-side across from the Kodak. A woman passes me as she exits the Guinness Museum. I hear her say, 'He lost five hundred and seventy pounds? I've been losing the same ten for the past twenty years!'

Here I am, back where I started, standing with the riff-raff on the *outside*.

No more stalling. It's time to suck it up and call Keith.

Just as I'm reaching into my pocket for my cell, I catch my reflection in the museum window.

'Hey, wait a minute,' I say, out loud.

There's still one avenue I haven't tried. The *hotel*. Where Ted is sitting in his air-conditioned limo. Where the brightest stars in the world are checking in. Where the 'press room' is really a conference room on the second floor. I missed the obvious! How hard could it be to walk into a hotel and take the elevator up two flights? I'll approach the press room from the rear!

Of course, security will still keep me out without a press pass. But I'll ask for Nell. When she comes out, I'll suggest having a massage therapist waiting for her at the Venice hotel. I'll mention that I saw Felicity Huffman and tell Nell that her body is *way* better. She'll clap her hands like a little kid. Then I'll casually mention that my lanyard broke and my press pass slipped off.

'While I was calling Venice to check on Stella,' I'll say, for added impact. 'She misses you, by the way.'

Nell will quickly get me a replacement so I can make her afternoon tea.

Brilliant! Keith never needs to know.

Off I go, in another wide circle around the barricades, stepping on the stars of Spencer Tracy, Danny Kaye and Claudette Colbert. Where, I wonder, are the Walk of Fame stars for Johnny Depp, Heath Ledger and Jude Law?

All of a sudden, the weight of my long day presses down on me. My feet feel as though I'm wearing cement shoes. The slight incline of Highland Avenue is Mount Everest. I've heard about flight fatigue, but never actually *felt* it before. Now, as I drag my arse to the Renaissance Hotel, I know what they mean by 'jet lag'. Even my eyeballs feel weighted down.

'Dig deep, Susanna,' I say, rubbing blood back into my cheeks. 'You can do it.'

I have to. Failure is not an option.

FIFTEEN

I fail instantly. The hotel's circular entrance is lined with limos. The pedestrian walkway is lined with cops. If I thought getting into the Kodak Theatre was impossible, it's nothing compared to the security overload surrounding the hotel where every major star in the world will sleep that night.

'Pardon me,' I say to one of the police officers blocking the path. My head is so heavy I can barely lift it. 'How do I get in there?'

Too tired to be creative, I go for the direct approach.

'You don't,' he says, gruffly. Apparently, he has jet lag, too.

'But I have to.'

'Too bad.'

'There's no way?' I ask.

'No way.'

'None?'

'*None.*'

97

Catching me completely by surprise, I burst into tears.

'I ... I ... lost my pass!' I wail. And the whole story comes spewing out. Along with, I'm mortified to discover, a small trickle of snot.

'And I don't have a tissue!' I sob.

The officer reaches into his back pocket and produces a handkerchief.

'Here,' he says, handing it to me.

Though I totally don't get the concept of blowing your nose in *fabric*, I'm desperate. I blow. I also sob, sniff, blubber and actually bury my head in his chest.

'I'm at the end of my rope,' I cry. 'And it wasn't a very long rope to begin with.'

'Come here,' he says.

Like the gates of Oz opening, the officer creates a space between two barricades large enough for my butt to squeeze through.

'I ... I ... don't know what to say,' I snivel. 'Thank you so much.'

'No problem, miss.'

My spirits lifted, I sniff hard and squeeze through the barricades. Finally, I'm back where I belong – on the *inside*. Looking up, I see the beautiful Renaissance Hotel. The red carpet is again beneath my feet. It's the 'yellow brick road' to my heart's desire. Purple and pink flowers reach their petals up to embrace me. The golden sun shines on my face. Smiling, I march for the lobby of my destiny.

'Where are you going?' the officer asks, his hand clamped on my shoulder.

'Going?' I blink. 'To the elevators. To the second floor.'

'You can't go in there.'

'But, you—'

'I let you through the barricades, miss, so you could pull yourself together.'

How can I pull anything together, I think, when my future just fell apart?

'Take a seat on that retaining wall,' he says, pointing. 'I'll get you some water.'

As directed, I sit. My tears have completely dried up. My nose is dry, too. Still clutching the officer's handkerchief, I notice the last remnants of my mascara smudged onto the white linen. An eerie calm overtakes me. A sense of resignation. This must be how a wild horse feels when the bit's between his teeth and the saddle is on his back and he's too tired to buck any more.

'Thanks.'

The officer hands me a cool plastic bottle of water. As I drink it, I tilt my face up to the sun. Who cares about a stupid sunburn when I'm a total loser?

I watch the crowd of tourists press against the barricade, cameras in hand. Someone important has arrived. I don't even care who it is.

'Do you mind if I make a phone call?' I ask the officer.

'Be my guest.'

Scrolling down the list of numbers I programmed into my cell before I left New York, I find Keith's. Why postpone the inevitable? It's time to confess and face the music.

'Keith?'

He picks up on the second ring.

'Where are you?' he asks.

'In front of the Renaissance Hotel,' I say, my voice quivering. 'On a retaining wall.'

'Good.'

'Good?'

Keith says, 'Get off the retaining wall and find Ted. Nell wants to head back to Venice. Sasha and I are going to stay here.'

I take a deep breath. 'Keith,' I begin, 'there's something I need to tell you.'

'Tell me later. Right now, Nell wants you to go to Venice with her.'

'Why me?' I swallow hard.

'Nell's motives are a mystery to us all, Susanna. Now get Ted, get the limo, and get going.'

I thank the police officer by giving him back his snotty handkerchief. It doesn't seem right, but what can I do? Buy him a new one? Without flinching, he tucks it in his pants pocket and escorts me back through the barricades.

'Have a nice day,' he says.

In spite of myself, I laugh. It must be all the sun in LA. It creates sunny personalities. Even though I've given him a pocket full of snot, the police officer is polite and kind.

'Thank you,' I reply, sincerely.

Ted, standing with other limo drivers, stamps out his cigarette the moment he sees me coming.

'Is my phone off?' he asks, alarmed.

'No,' I say. 'I was in the neighbourhood.'

Our limousine is fifth in a line of five limos. Ted opens the passenger door.

'Where are we going?' he asks.

'Back to the Venice hotel with Nell. But will you please pop the trunk first?'

The least I can do is freshen up for my boss. Though my comb and gloss are gone, I have Chapstick and a hairclip in my backpack. It's not much, but it's the best I can do.

Reaching under the driver's seat, Ted pulls a lever and the trunk pops open. He then starts the ignition and turns on the air-conditioning. His radio is set on a talk station.

Of course, my backpack is deep within the enormous trunk. Why should anything be easy today? In fact, it's the only thing in the trunk. Ted must have stopped short at a light on his way to the hotel, because my pack is so far in the trunk, I have to climb in to reach it.

The trunk is immaculate; the grey carpeting freshly vacuumed. It smells of vanilla. I'm now so tired I long to stretch out and take a nap on it. As I grab my pack, I clearly hear the talk show on the radio inside the car.

'Who are the Academy Members anyway?' the caller asks. 'And how can we be sure they aren't just voting for their friends?'

I chuckle as I lumber out of the trunk, my pack in hand.

Then I stop. I look around and feel a power surge race through my body.

'My God,' I say out loud. 'I've got it!'

Ted suddenly appears at the back of the car.

'What's wrong?' he asks. 'Why are you sitting in my trunk?'

I open my mouth, then I close it right away.

'For the first time today,' I say, hopping out, 'everything is totally *right*. I've just figured out how to get my scoop.'

SIXTEEN

'He's here.'

Sighing, Nell presses her white-blonde head against the limo window. Her Prada bag is in a heap on the leather seat next to her. Her ivory linen pants are a wrinkled mess. Ted is driving us both back to the beach.

'Who's here?' I ask, gingerly. Though I really want to ask, 'Why am *I* here?' I have serious planning to do before tomorrow.

'With his wife,' Nell moans. 'That actress.'

I have no idea who she's talking about, but I've never seen Nell Wickham so deflated. She looks ... almost normal. The dark circles under her eyes are visible, and her skin is as blotchy as mine. Ted turns left on Highland Avenue, then a quick right on Franklin.

'Do you want a martini?' I ask Nell, not sure how to handle this shift in the cosmic order.

'No thanks, luv,' she says to me.

Luv? Now I'm sure the end of the world is near.

As Ted passes the famed corner of Hollywood and Vine, heading for the ocean, I sit quietly and shift my focus back to getting the scoop of the century. In fact, I now know how to get the scoop of the *millennium*. I just have no idea how to actually *get* it. I mean, I know what I want to do, but how, exactly, do you do it?

'It's my own fault,' Nell says, quietly. 'Who knows how many other middle-aged women's lives I've ruined? It's against nature. You can't fight nature forever and get away with it. I deserve this.'

Suddenly, I'm listening. Nell Wickham accepting blame? Nell believing she deserves something other than five-hundred-dollar shoes and fresh flowers every morning? Anything but lilacs, which, she claims, smell like 'old ladies'. Yes, the Universe is definitely spinning out of control.

'How much does the average American woman weigh, Sue?' Nell asks, looking directly at me. I blush magenta.

'I don't know,' I mutter, silently praying it's way more than my scale reading that morning. How much does a roast beef sandwich weigh?

'One hundred and forty-two pounds,' Nell says. 'Five feet, four inches.'

I exhale, relieved.

'Models are six feet tall and under one twenty,' she continues.

If I was over six feet tall, I think, my weight would be *perfect*.

'The average age of an American woman is forty-four,' Nell moans. 'Do you know how old models are?'

'Younger.'

'Most start in their teens and end their careers in their twenties. And actresses, well, they have the shelf life of cottage cheese. Not so with men. Turn on the telly and you'll see middle-aged husbands married to thin, young, beautiful wives. It's worse here in America, but it's a problem everywhere. And I'm to blame.'

Isn't she taking this 'responsibility' thing too far? I mean, she didn't cast Carrie opposite Doug on *The King of Queens*, or Judy opposite Bill on *Still Standing*. And has the woman never watched *The OC*? Everyone is thin and beautiful on that show.

'I've spent my adult life creating glossy magazine pages full of beautiful people,' Nell says. 'If an actress gains ten pounds, we print the ghastly photos. But when Harrison hooked up with Calista, and Jack with Lara, did anyone call them lecherous, flabby old men? Did we print close-ups of their bald spots and paunches? No! I deserve everything I get. I've glorified the culture of youth and beauty and now it's biting me in my sagging bum.'

Ted glances sympathetically at me in the rear-view mirror. I can't stand it any longer.

'What *happened*, Nell?' I ask.

My boss sighs extravagantly. She bites her lip and says, 'I just saw the love of my life with his stunning, young actress wife.'

'Who?'

'Names aren't important. The fact is, he barely looked at me. He looked *through* me. Like I'm nobody.'

'But you're Nell Wickham!' I blurt out.

She smiles the saddest smile I've ever seen. I actually feel sorry for her. For Queen *Nell*. The royal pain in the arse.

'I'm old and wrinkled and fat,' she says.

'You're not, not and not!' I reply, patting her shoulder. For the first time, I feel compassion for the woman who said last summer, 'Why don't those starving Africans just move to a town that has more food?'

Nell's pathetic look makes me almost like her.

'I have an idea,' she says, trying to smile. 'When we get back to the hotel, Susan, let's have a picnic!'

A *picnic*? My gulp is audible. I said I *almost* liked her.

'Order one of those big, sloppy American pizzas. With peppercorns.'

106

'Peppercorns?'

'You know, those round, red, greasy things you Americans love to eat.'

'Pepper*oni*,' I say.

'Yes! We'll eat pizza and drink beer and the whole lot can sod off.'

Ted gives me another look in the rear-view mirror. He raises his eyebrows as if to say, 'You're in for it now.'

What can I do? She's my boss. For better, worse and pepperoni.

'Great,' I say. 'Do you like garlic knots?'

By the time the pizza arrives at the Venice Beach House Hotel, Nell has changed her mind *and* her personality. When I knock on her door to announce dinnertime, she opens it only wide enough to let Stella and her leash out.

'Feed her, too,' she commands, 'after she's been to the loo.' Then she slams the door in my face.

It's barely five o'clock. I shrug my shoulders. For the rest of the night, Stella and I – plus a large pepperoni pizza and garlic knots – are on our own. I ask the hotel guy if he can keep my pizza warm in the oven, then Stella and I head for the beach.

Hey, it could be worse.

SEVENTEEN

Amazingly, the Venice Beach Boardwalk is exactly like it looks on TV. Rollerbladers zigzag back and forth, reggae music blares from boom boxes, tiny storefronts selling sunglasses and junk line the east side of the sandy pathway. As Stella and I walk, the salt air revives me. My jet lag has morphed into a sort of weary excitement. The white sand and fading sunlight are beyond beautiful. Instantly, I understand why Nell insisted on staying near the ocean. Just hearing the gentle sound of lapping waves makes me feel peaceful.

'On your left!' A cyclist glides by us on a bicycle built for reclining. It even has a cushioned backrest! Stella barks at it.

'We're not in New York any more, Toto,' I say to her.

The smell of rubber and sweat fills the air as we approach Muscle Beach – the outdoor gym where buffed and bulging guys grunt as they lift enormous weights. I see palm trees swaying in the light breeze and bums asleep on a patch of bright green lawn.

'Want your name written on a grain of rice?' a woman asks me as she sits behind a table on the boardwalk. 'It makes a beautiful necklace or keychain.'

Intrigued, I stop.

'What if I have a long name, like Susanna?'

She laughs. 'I'll use long-grain rice.'

I'm tempted to buy one for Amelia. She'd definitely think it was cool. And my parents did give me fifty dollars 'for emergencies'. But I think twice. Besides the fact that my whole *day* has been an emergency, tomorrow is do-or-die time. Who knows how many crises lie ahead?

'No, thanks,' I say. Stella and I walk on.

I have serious work to do.

A plan to hatch.

A face to save.

One thing I know for sure: I need two pieces of equipment to do what I need to do – a flashlight and a cheap tape recorder. Without them, I might as well be any ordinary teen intern without a press pass who's squandered the biggest opportunity of her life.

EIGHTEEN

Here I am. Staring at my reflection in the bathroom mirror across from my Tramp's Quarters in the hotel.

My Confessional.

I'm sitting here spilling my guts.

'Mom is going to kill me,' I say out loud, noticing my sunburned nose. Grabbing a tissue, I soak it in cool water and lay it on my hot skin. Then I grab a slice of pizza and resume my confession.

'Okay.'

Inhaling deeply, I hold it a moment before blowing the hot air out. But it does nothing to calm the squirrels in my stomach. A bite of spicy pepperoni doesn't help much, either. Especially since it's *LA* pizza which is majorly inferior to the NY variety. They call this a crust?

While Stella and I were out, I bought a flashlight and a tape recorder. I also ran through what I needed to pull off the plan of the century. Namely: guts.

'The Nike approach,' I say out loud. 'Just do it.'

If it works, I'll be a hero. If it doesn't, I'll be a heel. Or worse, a felon. My heart hammers against my ribcage. The stakes couldn't be higher.

'This is no time to wimp out, Susanna,' I say into the mirror. 'No risk, no reward, right? Okay, here's the deal the limos will all be in front of the hotel by, say, three o'clock.'

I take another bite. 'That gives me an—'

Someone knocks on the door.

'Yes?' I say, swallowing quickly.

'Who's in there with you?'

It's Nell. There's no mistaking her British accent and the terror her voice instantly inflicts on me.

'No one,' I say.

'Your parents made me promise to take care of you,' she says. 'I won't have you fooling around.'

I nearly burst into laughter. Nell didn't even notice I was wandering the streets of Venice alone. Now that I'm safely locked in a bathroom, she's freaking out?

Wiping tomato sauce off my lips with the damp tissue I remove from my nose, I unlock the door and let Nell see for herself.

'Just me,' I say.

'What's that awful stench?'

My eyes go wide. Panicked, my first thought is that

I actually used the bathroom for its intended purpose. Then I realise, no, I haven't. All I've been doing is talking to myself in the mirror and eating pizza.

'Pepperoni,' I say, abruptly.

Nell makes a face. 'No wonder all you Americans are obese.'

Hurt, I'm tempted to remind her that her ex-boyfriend's current actress wife is tiny and fit. But I don't know who she is, exactly. For all I know, she may be French. I also want to tell my boss that I'm not *large*, I'm big-boned. Between the two of us, I'd definitely survive longer on a desert island.

'I'm feeling peckish,' Nell says, before I can formulate any actual words.

'Pizza?' I ask, pointing towards the open box teetering on the edge of the bathtub.

'God, no,' Nell replies. 'Order me some sushi, will you? No, make that sashimi. I don't want a rice bloat tomorrow.'

With that, she turns to leave. Then she instantly turns back around.

'I almost forgot,' she says. 'Keith asked me to give you this.'

Before my eyes, Nell Wickham pulls my press pass out of her pocket.

113

My jaw hits the tile floor.

'Where did you find it?!' I screech joyfully.

'A security guard stumbled on it and returned it to the press room this afternoon. Really, Susie, you should be more careful.'

'Yes!' I squeal. 'I should!'

'He found this lipgloss, too. If it's yours, throw it out. The colour is hideous.'

'It's mine. I will!'

I'm so happy, I want to plant a greasy pepperoni kiss right on Nell's lips. But she's already back down the hall to her suite. This has to be a good omen! My plan will work perfectly tomorrow! Skipping downstairs, I ask the hotel owner how to order the best non-bloating sashimi in town.

NINETEEN

The sun wakes me up. For a moment, I have no idea where I am. The floral quilt in the Tramp's Quarters is twisted around my body like a cocoon. Suddenly, I remember.

It's *today*.

Today is the day I, Susanna Barringer, show the whole world how it's done. *If* I can untangle myself from this bedspread.

'Good morning.'

Keith and Sasha are downstairs in the dining room eating breakfast. I smell fresh coffee and hot cinnamon buns. If I wasn't so nervous, I'd be starved. But, at this moment, I feel like an Oscar nominee. In a few short hours, my fate will be decided.

'Please tell me that's not what you're planning to wear,' Sasha says.

My cheeks go red. I was hoping Sasha would approve.

Admittedly, my Oscar-night outfit was a dilemma. I mean, I wasn't about to buy a gown. And, when I asked Sasha if she had any possibilities from *Scene*'s fashion closet – similar to the Jeffrey Chow she scored for me to wear to Randall Sanders' movie premiere last summer – she just laughed.

'You're *working*,' she said.

I'd been working that night, too. Even though 'working' meant gawking at everybody and telling Keith and Nell what I saw.

'What's wrong with this dress?' I ask Sasha as she pokes a spoon into half a grapefruit.

'You're not a bridesmaid, Susanna. This is the Academy Awards!'

I'm crushed. It took me hours to pick out this outfit. Mom let me use her Bloomie's discount and I tried nearly everything on in the store before selecting the most flattering look.

'Pink is *so* last year,' Sasha says.

Sasha is decked out in a long, white, strapless Goddess gown.

'White totally washes me out,' I say.

Shaking her head, Sasha asks, 'Did you bring black pants?'

'Pants?' I say. 'On Oscar night?'

Keith laughs. 'Are you up for some award you haven't told us about? Best Performance by an Intern?'

'Ha, ha,' I say. 'I just thought—'

'Unless you're a presenter, nominee, or the host,' Sasha says, 'it's a regular day at work. You want to blend in, not make Cojo's worst-dressed list.'

My eyebrow lifts at the sight of Sasha's designer gown. Blend in?

'I'm working the red carpet,' she says, reading my mind. 'I have to look hot. You don't.'

That's what you think, I want to say. Number one, I'll be spending the day with Keith. Number two, Randall Sanders will be there. Number three, I'll be inches away from every star in Hollywood. *You* dress like this is just another day at work!

What I *actually* say is, 'I'll find something in my suitcase,' and return to the Tramp's Quarters.

On my way up the stairs, I pass Nell.

'Shouldn't you be out of your nightgown, Suzanne?' she says. 'We leave any minute!'

Wardrobe is the least of my problems. Tired as I was, I barely slept at all last night. No wonder I woke up wrapped in a comforter. Some comfort! High anxiety had me rolling like a sausage sizzling in a frying pan. Today is

117

D-Day and I'm still not entirely sure how to pull off my Master Plan without getting caught.

Best to take it one step at a time, I say to myself. First step: find something sophisticated, chic, slimming and stylish in my high-schooler's suitcase.

Clearly, I only have one choice: my favourite flared-leg black pants, a black tank and the purple velveteen mini blazer I bought at the Gap. Thank God I dug my platform sandals out of winter storage. Sneakers would totally ruin the look.

'Better,' Sasha says, as I return to the breakfast room.

Then she grabs a cup of black coffee and disappears up the stairs. Nell and Keith soon follow, leaving me alone with a breakfast buffet and a stomach full of butterflies.

'Mom?' I use these few extra moments to call my parents on my cell.

'Why haven't you called me?' Mom asks.

'I'm calling right now.'

'I was waiting by my phone yesterday.'

'Yesterday was, uh, *busy*.' That's all my mother needs to know about the Susanna Streep fiasco.

Mom says, 'I didn't want to call you in case you were in the middle of something important.'

'I was,' I say, careful *not* to mention my search for the

VIP loo. 'It's been incredibly exciting.' Before she can ask me to elaborate, I ask her, 'How are The Trips?'

'Sam looked for you all over the apartment. I showed him California on the globe and he licked it.'

I laugh. Mom asks, 'Are you warm?'

'I am.'

'Are you rubbing elbows with Hollywood's elite?'

'Tom Hanks waved at me yesterday,' I say.

'Is Nell taking good care of you?'

'Yes, Mom. Everything is good.'

'I'm glad it's all working out, honey,' she says.

I flash on my lost-and-found press pass, my exile beyond the barricades, my sunburned nose, Nell's meltdown yesterday, my dress disaster that morning, today's insane plan, and I say, 'Yeah. Me, too.'

'Go get 'em, honey,' Mom says, blowing a kiss into the phone.

Fingers crossed, that's exactly what I plan to do.

TWENTY

Nell emerges from the Venice Beach House Hotel in a white silk pantsuit. Keith has thrown a cream-coloured jacket over his open-necked pale pink shirt. Sasha looks awesome in her pleated white chiffon gown. As I clomp down the stairs in my black and purple 'working' outfit, I feel like a crow in a flock of doves.

'Relax, Susanna,' Keith says. 'It's only the Academy Awards.'

My heart is pounding so hard, I'm quite sure it'll burst free from my chest and bounce down Hollywood Boulevard. As we near the Kodak Theatre, I catch my first glimpse of the spectacle I'm about to enter. Today's scene is like yesterday's scene – but on *steroids*. Everything is pumped up. The air itself is supercharged. There are lights, cameras, action. The police force is doubled. The crowd is tripled. Clutching my press pass as it dangles around my neck, I turn to Keith and mouth the word, 'Wow.'

Right now, that's all I *can* say.

The sidewalk lining Hollywood Boulevard has been transformed into one long red carpet. The crowd reminds me of Times Square on New Year's Eve. No one seems to care how long they've stood in the sun. Eventually, the long hours will pay off.

Ted shows his driver's pass to the officer guarding the street in front of the golden archway. As he pulls up, we drive into bright television lights. The archway shimmers like a solid gold rainbow. Oscar, standing proudly beside it, glows. His chest juts forward. For the first time, I notice that he's holding a sword. He's also standing on a reel of film.

One by one, we get out of the limo. Cameras flash in our faces even though Nell is the only recognisable celebrity. The crowd is screaming so loudly, I can't hear a word they're saying.

'You forgot your backpack, Susanna!' Ted calls to me from the limousine's trunk.

'I don't need it right now,' I shout over the noise. 'Could you please leave it in the trunk?'

Nodding, Ted tosses my pack in the trunk and slams it shut. Then he returns to the driver's seat and disappears down the road.

The red carpet leading into the Kodak Theatre is crawling with men and women in black.

'Who are these people?' I ask Keith.

'Publicists, mostly,' he says. 'And ushers. When a star steps out of the limo, the publicist is at his side, making sure he talks to the right reporters and doesn't goof off with his friends. Make no mistake, Susanna, the red carpet is *work*, for everyone involved. If a star looks bad, or, God forbid, has nipples showing through her dress, the publicists will have hell to pay.'

I think back to Drew Barrymore's majorly booby dress at the Golden Globe Awards a couple of years ago and wonder, did her publicist ask her to put on a bra?

'C'mon inside,' Keith shouts. 'We have work to do.'

'Aren't you going to take any photos?' I ask.

'Red carpet spots are reserved for a precious few. The rest of us buy photos from them. If they let every media outlet on the red carpet, there would be no room for the stars.'

'Ah,' I say. It makes sense. The publicists alone are taking up most of the space!

'Sasha will be out here getting quotes. Nell will be inside enjoying the show, and you and I will be in the press room hearing over and over how heavy the statuette is and how it really *was* an honour just to be nominated.'

Laughing, I follow Keith Franklin through the metal detector, up the staircase to the second-floor press room, where I try and figure out how to gracefully ask Keith for a couple of hours off.

TWENTY-ONE

As it was outside, the press room is buzzing. I still hear all the languages of the world, but the voices are louder, the hand movements larger, the outfits more deliberate.

'Here's how things are going to go once the show starts,' Keith begins. 'That door will open, a star will come sweeping through, and every photographer's camera will be clicking like mad.'

'Uh-huh,' I say, nodding.

'The publicist will hand out press information on the winner. You take what they give you and jot down any answers to questions that we might want to publish.'

'Okay.'

He hands me a Polaroid camera. 'This is for writers, costume designers, producers, special effects – anyone you don't immediately recognise. Take their photo with the Polaroid and attach it to the press material. Got it?'

'Got it,' I say.

'We want to be able to identify them later. Don't make a mistake.'

'I won't,' I say, my mouth getting dry again.

'Finally, Susanna, if you feel like asking a question, resist. This is no time to get your scoop.'

Keith stops for a moment, then asks, 'How did it go yesterday, by the way?'

'Great!' I lie.

'Even after you lost your press pass?'

He grins. I try to resist those dimples in the same way I plan to resist asking my favourite stars the questions I've been dying to know all my life.

'Admittedly, things got a little less great after that,' I say.

Keith asks, 'Do you have any questions about your job tonight?'

Questions? My heart resumes its hip-hop routine in my chest.

'Uh,' I tiptoe in, 'according to the schedule Carmen gave me, the first award is presented about five-thirty, right?'

'Right.'

'I was wondering—' I try to swallow. Nothing goes down. Nike approach – just do it, Susanna. 'Do you think maybe I could have an hour or two off?'

'Off?' Keith bursts out laughing. 'You want to check out the Wax Museum?'

Quickly, I pull Keith away from the other reporters.

'I have an idea,' I whisper.

'Uh-oh.'

'I swear to you, I'll be in the press room by the time the show starts.'

'Susanna, what's going on?'

'Nothing illegal, grossly immoral or embarrassing to the magazine,' I say.

Keith narrows his eyes.

'It's better if you don't know,' I add.

Staring at me so long I blush, Keith finally says, 'Know who you remind me of?'

'Who?'

'Me. When I was just starting out, there was no stopping me, either.'

'So you'll let me go?' I ask, hopeful.

'Is there any stopping you?'

Lifting my head, I look directly into Keith's cobalt-blue eyes.

'You've given me the chance of a lifetime,' I say. 'I'm at the Academy Awards! If you need me to stand here next to you all day and night, I will. I'll get you coffee and sandwiches and take Polaroids and not ask a single question. I'll do whatever you need me to do. But—' I take a deep breath. 'If you can spare me for an hour or two, I may be able to give you even more.'

Keith Franklin's curly eyelashes lower over his eyes. When they come up, they're nearly touching his brows.

'Go for it,' he says.

For the second time in two days, I throw my arms around Keith's neck. This time, he kisses my cheek. His lips *are* as soft as they look.

'Be back by four,' he says, wagging his finger at me. 'With a *scoop*.'

TWENTY-TWO

There's an old Chinese expression my father always says: 'Be careful what you wish for, you may get it.' For the first time, I totally get why it's a warning. Keith has given me the green light and I feel like I'm going to hurl.

'Get a grip, Susanna,' I say out loud, as I walk back down the stairs, under the golden archway, past Oscar, and across the red carpet. The stars will be arriving in an hour or two. This is my last shot.

With my platform sandals clomping down Hollywood Boulevard, my press pass flapping against my chest, I try not to hyperventilate. My heart is still racing, but there's no turning back now. As I pass Grauman's Chinese Theatre, the crowd sounds fade. There, in the sidewalk cement, I see Eddie Murphy's handprints and footprints. Next to his signature, he wrote the words, 'Be free'.

'Be *brave*,' I say out loud. Then I bite my lip and try not to barf.

At Orange Avenue, on the west side of the huge

Hollywood and Highland Center, I turn right. The citrus trees overhead are lush and green. The sweet smell of orange is in the air. At the very last tree, just before the circular Orange Court Drive, I launch the first part of my plan. I pull my cell phone out of my pocket and call Ted.

'Susanna?' He picks up on the second ring.

'Hi, Ted,' I say, talking slowly to calm my voice.

'What's up?'

One more deep breath, then I dive in.

'You know my boss is nuts, right?' I say.

Ted laughs. 'I've noticed a few quirks.'

'Well, here's the latest. She took a walk over to the Orange Court. You know, on Orange Avenue?'

'I know where it is.'

'She, um, wants you to pick her up.'

'And take her where?' Ted asks.

'Back to the front of the Kodak.'

Now Ted howls. 'She knows I'm working the red carpet arrivals, right?'

'Yeah,' I say, wincing.

'I'm already in the limo line in front of the hotel.'

'I know,' I say. 'It won't take long.'

Sighing, Ted says, 'All right. Tell her I'll be there in five minutes.'

'Ted?'

'Yes?'

'Don't flip out – there's one more thing.'

'What?'

I swallow hard.

'I know this is going to sound bizarre, but here is what Nell wants you to do. Pull into the circular driveway, leave the air-conditioner on, and meet her in the courtyard. If she's not there in five minutes, you can head back to the hotel.'

'*What?!*'

'She's totally stressed out about some personal stuff, and may decide to walk back herself.'

Ted groans. 'That woman is certifiable.'

'I'm sorry,' I say.

'Don't sweat it, Susanna. It's not your fault.'

Guilt slumps my shoulders.

'Thank you, Ted,' I say, as we both hang up.

Of course, it's *totally* my fault All of it. But I'm not lying, I tell myself again, I'm going *undercover*. And, covering up the truth is the best way to protect Ted, Keith and Nell. What they don't know, won't hurt them. Plus, what they don't know, they can't refuse to let me do.

There's no turning back now. My plan is in motion.

Switching my cell to 'vibrate', I look for a place to hide. Which isn't as easy as I thought it would be. Yesterday, when I walked past the Orange Court, it was swarming with people. Today, everyone is around the corner, on the red carpet, trying to catch a glimpse of a star. The Orange Court is deserted.

Ahead, I spot a high bush at the base of an orange tree. There's a retaining wall there, too. Thank God I didn't wear a dress! Leaping over the wall, I crouch down behind the bush. Leaving the lanyard around my neck, I tuck my press pass securely into my Infinity Edge bra. My toes feel the coolness of the ivy I'm now standing in.

I'm inches away from freaking out.

As every New Yorker knows, *rats* love ivy. They scuttle beneath those green leaves, invisible to anyone who can't spot the tell-tale leaf flicker. I can *always* spot the flicker. And I'm looking for it right now.

Suddenly, out of the corner of my eye, I detect movement. I see a flash of black. It's no rat, it's Ted, in the limo. As instructed, he pulls up in front of the courtyard, leaves the car running, then steps out to find Nell. The moment he's out of sight, I make my move.

With the agility of an Olympic hurdler, I fly over the wall and run to the driver's side door. My stomach is as tight as a fist. Crouching low, I open the door just wide enough to reach in and grab the lever. As soon as I hear the familiar *pop* of the trunk, I shut the door and scurry to the back of the limo. My heart is thumping so hard my press pass pops out of my bra. I shove it back in. And, with one final glance around to make sure no one is watching, I open the trunk, jump in, and slam it shut behind me.

I did it. I'm in.

Frozen with fear, I lie there, panting, waiting for someone to bang on the trunk and shout, 'Hey! What are you doing in there?'

But no one does. Amazingly, my plan is working so far. If only I could stop my heart from racing. Can a heart actually wear out? If so, mine will cramp up at any moment and collapse. It's never beaten so hard in its life.

As soon as I gather my wits, I crawl on my elbows to the very front of the trunk and wait. It's dark. I smell exhaust. *Chill*, I say to myself. This is no time to have a claustrophobic freak-out. I feel around for my backpack and pull out the flashlight. As expected, my cell phone eventually vibrates. I know it's Ted, telling me that Nell is nowhere to be found. But I can't risk answering it in here. He'll have to leave a message.

Just then, I feel the car dip slightly. I switch off the flashlight as I hear the driver's side door slam. Instantly, we're on the move. The car rolls beneath my stomach. My body shifts slightly to the left as Ted turns right. In the dark, in the trunk, up on my elbows, I silently clap my hands together. So far, so good. By the time Ted gets back in the limo line in front of the hotel and picks up his first celebrity, I'll have my tape recorder ready, and my first instalment of Susanna Barringer's *Limousine Confessions* on the way.

TWENTY-THREE

It's hot in here. At least the limo's trunk is huge, so I can breathe. If the air gets too stale, there's a release lever that will let me out. It'll be mortifying, to say the least, to pop open the trunk and tumble out onto the red carpet. But it's comforting to know I can, if I need to.

Way up by the driver's seat, I hear a muffled voice. 'Pull up, please.'

Ted replies, 'Sure thing.'

We pull up.

As I shine the flashlight on my watch, I see that the stars will be streaming out of the Hollywood Renaissance Hotel soon, dressed in gowns and tuxes, dripping in diamonds, their hair professionally coiffed, their make-up applied perfectly. I'd give anything to see them, but I'll have to settle for the next-best thing. Audio. An excellent plan, if I may say so myself. Yeah, it would be *awesome* to have a hidden limo cam on the way to the Academy Awards. But a hidden tape recorder is almost as good.

Who doesn't want to know what the stars are saying on their way to the biggest night of their lives?

I, Susanna Barringer, am going to tell the world via the pages of *Scene* magazine. Nell will be thrilled.

Brilliant!

Ted pulls up once more and I feel a rush of warm air as the passenger door opens. My heart lurches. Showtime! Though my palms are clammy, I keep my index finger perched on the 'record' button of the tape recorder I bought yesterday.

'Breathe, Susanna,' I remind myself each time my chest burns. 'In. Out.'

The limo bounces slightly four times as four people get in. Instantly, I smell perfume and hair products. *Expensive* hair stuff. Sisley Botanicals, probably. Someone asks, 'Ready?' A fifth bounce, and a faint door slam, let me know that Ted is in the driver's seat.

As softly as a snowflake falling, I press 'record'.

Away we go.

'Do I have lipstick on my teeth?' a female voice asks.

'Let me see,' another female replies.

'You look great,' a guy says. 'Relax.'

So far, I don't recognise any of the voices. A rather large crimp in my plan to capture a star's private conversation.

I mean, who wants to know what someone they don't know says?

'No way will I be able to sit in this dress for three hours,' the woman says. 'I'm already suffocating.'

'Your job is to look beautiful tonight, not to breathe,' the guy says.

Everyone laughs. The woman asks, 'Who can look beautiful in this harsh sunlight? The red carpet is a torture chamber.'

'God, I'm hungry,' the guy says.

'*You* are? I've been living on salad greens since the nominations were announced. The one thing I want more than the Oscar is a juicy cheeseburger.'

'No problem. We'll swing by In 'N' Out Burger on the way to the Governor's Ball.'

Chuckles all around.

The woman asks, 'Will you be following me around all night?'

A deep male voice says, 'Not you, exactly. But I will be following your necklace.'

Laughter again erupts in the limo. The other woman says, 'Every borrowed diamond tonight comes with its own bodyguard charm.'

'I'll try to be invisible,' says the deep voice.

I hear the crowd noise ramp up as Ted slows down.

'Here we go,' the other guy sings.

Nervously, the woman says, 'When I lose tonight, make sure you say something to me. I don't want that camera in my face all alone.'

'I'll talk to you if you lose only if you thank me *first* when you win.'

The door opens. Cheers swell. The nominee, her diamond necklace, its bodyguard, her husband or boyfriend and probably a publicist get out. The limo sways slightly with their exit. Then the door slams and it's quiet again as Ted circles around the block for his next pickup.

Silently, I press 'stop' on the recorder.

Driving a limo is like a box of chocolates, I remember Ted saying. *You never know who you're going to get.*

Man, is that ever true! I have no idea who we just drove to the Academy Awards. But it doesn't matter. I'll ask Ted later. Until then, I grin and sigh and lie flat on the soft floor of the trunk, waiting for my next piece of chocolate.

TWENTY-FOUR

It doesn't take long to circle back to the front of the hotel. The intermittent start and stop let me know that Ted is back in the limo line. Outside, I hear garbled orders, like someone is directing traffic.

Abruptly, the passenger door swings open.

Again, the limo sways as its passengers get in. This time, I feel three depressions. I smell perfume that I never smell at Macy's. Something spiced and sweet, like a cinnamon flower.

A male voice jokes, 'Home, James.'

I recognise it instantly. And when a female laughs and says, 'You want to go home when I spent two hours getting ready?' I know who they *both* are. Will and Jada! Hollywood's happiest couple. Filmdom's coolest hotties! The third passenger must be the diamond guard.

'Willow?' I hear Will say. 'Mommy and Daddy are almost there. You can turn on the TV now. When I wave at the camera, you and Jaden will know I'm waving just for you.'

Jada says, 'Trey, too.'

'And Trey, too. Make sure everybody waves back.'

I'm nearly bursting. How cool is this? Will Smith is in his limo on the way to the Academy Awards and he calls his daughter to tell her to watch and wave! Plus Jada, whom I can just picture in a skin-tight dress showing off her awesome biceps, includes Trey, Will's teenage son from his first marriage. Which is *so* like her. Jada made sure the family Will had when he was a 'Fresh Prince' was still part of their lives when Oscar came calling. Would I be generous enough to include Randall Sanders' ex in my life? Set a place for her at my Thanksgiving table? If I did, I'd be way too nervous to eat. Now that's one weight-loss plan I could stick to.

The limo slows down and I hear the roar of the crowd. I am *dying* to tell Will how fab he was in *Pursuit of Happyness*. But I bite my tongue and quietly press the 'stop' button on the tape recorder as soon as I feel the Smiths step out.

Will and Jada. *Wow*. I can't wait to hear who gets in next.

On the way back to the hotel, I think about Amelia. How fun would it be if she were here with me? Though

140

my best friend is definitely not the type to leap in a limo trunk. Not that many girls are. Except, of course, *moi*.

Ted stops, then starts again. Must be a red light, I think. Maybe 'Frankenstein's monster' is crossing the road?

Soon enough, we're back in the limo line – once again, lurching forward in small chunks. My heart sings as I hear the crowd call the name of the next star to go for a ride in our car.

'Drew! Drew!'

Could it be *that* Drew? *The* Drew? The door opens and two people get in. I hold my breath. God, I hope it's not comic Drew Carey. Not that there's anything wrong with him. It's just that a Carey would be a major disappointment when you're hoping for a Barrymore. Especially since I totally loved her in that poker movie with that smokin'-hot actor from *Munich*.

'I hope they have those same little chocolate Oscars as last year,' I hear Drew say. Yes! It's *the* Drew Barrymore. I silently cheer.

'Wolfgang Puck will do something awesome with the food at the after-party,' her companion says. I don't recognise him at all. Is he that guy in that band? Her half-brother, maybe? Tom Green? Are they still friends even though they're no longer married?

Drew says, 'That was real gold they were dipped in!'

'We ate gold?'

'Did it taste like chicken to you?'

Drew giggles. I laugh, too. Inside. Plus, it takes all the willpower I can muster not to push through the divider between the trunk and the seat to see if Drew is wearing a bra. Is she still brunette, I wonder? Or back to blonde? Really, she has a blonde personality. But in a *good* way.

They don't say much the rest of the way. But, when Ted stops the limo and Drew and her mystery style rise out of the car, I sigh happily. How many high-schoolers can say they were inches away from Drew Barrymore? And I'm dying to taste real gold.

On the way back to the hotel, feeling the road rumble beneath me, I lie on my back and stretch out in the huge trunk. A surge of pride fills my chest. By far, this is the greatest idea I've ever had.

The rhythm of the limo trips soon becomes a relaxing cruise. Maybe it's the lack of fresh air, but I feel completely chilled out. The only thing that would make this under-cover operation more comfortable would be a burger and fries. Ever since that first passenger – whoever she was – mentioned her craving for a juicy cheeseburger, I've been wanting to swing by an In 'N' Out Burger, too. Though I have no idea what it is. Still, if a star eats there, it has to be good.

142

'Thanks, man.'

My next passenger, as I've come to see them – *mine* – has one of the most unmistakable voices in Hollywood. It's Owen Wilson! I'd know that nasal twang anywhere.

He climbs in the limo with one other person. Is it his brother Luke? His other brother, Andrew? Is it that girl he met at Venice Beach? I can't remember – is she the stripper or the salsa dancer?

Though my tape recorder rolls, Owen and his mystery date don't say a word. Are they making out? I wiggle closer to the front of the truck to see if I can hear lips smacking. Then I stop and roll my eyes. No way would any woman allow a guy to kiss her in the limo on the way to Oscar night! What am I thinking? They'd emerge in front of the world's press with lipstick smears all over their faces!

'Thanks, man,' Owen says again, as he gets out. I hear the crowd cheer, and I long to cheer, too. He was hilarious in *Night at the Museum*. That scruffy blond head and crooked nose are irresistible. If my heart didn't already belong to Randall Sanders, Owen Wilson would definitely be in the running. Right behind Adrian Grenier of *Entourage* and the latest addition to my list of 'Actors I Could Watch All Day': Dominic Cooper, the hottest hottie of *The History Boys*. If I was in his class, I'd *never* be able to pay attention to the teacher.

On the way back to the hotel, I switch on the flashlight to check my watch. My heart sinks. Man, time flies when you're circling Hollywood in a trunk! I promised Keith I'd be back in the press room by four and it's getting dangerously close. So far, my *Limousine Confessions* are incredibly tame. Why can't Whitney and Bobby be thrown together? Or Jude and Sienna? Are they on or off? I need some *spice*. An actress with a rip in her dress, or an actor who had too much champagne in the hotel bar. Maybe that boy-bander who came out as gay. Did he have a former girlfriend?

I know it's not very compassionate, but I've watched 'Confession' shows enough to know they only air the saucy stuff. If I produce a tape full of fluff, Nell will toss it out as quickly as she'll toss me Stella's leash. My budding career as a celebrity reporter will fade into a blur of poop scoops.

'If you wrinkle my tux, I'll kill you.'

The next passenger gets in. It's a man. I don't recognise his voice. My spirits sag into the soft carpet beneath my belly. I feel two more people get in. Crossing my fingers, I hold my breath.

That's when I hear it.

'Ooh ah hah hah!'

Her laugh is unmistakable. It's so clear, I can almost see her wide smile, white teeth, and twinkling brown eyes. I'm about to explode. Julia Roberts is in my limo!

Of course, she would say that I'm in *her* limo, but why quibble over words when one of the biggest stars in the world is inches away?

Julia sounds totally relaxed, giggly and happy. That must be her handsome husband with her! And a publicist? A diamond bodyguard? Her brother? What do I care? I'm about to capture the limousine confession of Julia Roberts. I can barely keep myself from whooping with joy. Slowly, I press my finger on the 'record' button and try not to squeal.

That's when I hear another voice.

It's male. Outside the car. Way up front, by the driver.

This voice says four words that chill my blood.

'Random security check, sir.'

My eyes shoot open. What, exactly, does that mean? The limo isn't moving. Are they checking Julia Roberts' handbag?

Quickly, I press the 'stop button' on the tape recorder, as if that's the only incriminating evidence against me. Then, panicked, and with no better idea, I shut my eyes, curl up on the trunk's carpet and try to disappear.

'What the—?'

Sunlight suddenly floods my cave. I don't move. In a flurry of uniforms and walkie-talkies and gasps, I'm poked and prodded to make sure I'm alive. Squinting, I roll over, pretending to be awakened from a deep sleep.

'Oh, hi,' I say, rubbing my eyes.

'Susanna?'

Ted is one of the heads peering at me from the trunk's opening.

'You know this girl?' the security guard asks him.

'Yes.' Then he turns to me and asks the obvious question. 'What are you doing in there?'

'Here?' I stall. A thousand lame explanations flash through my brain.

I'm hiding from Nell.

I'm avoiding sunburn.

Did you get a ransom note?

In the stress of the moment, I settle on the lamest explanation of all.

'I left my backpack in trunk,' I say. 'Before I could reach it, the limo started moving.'

Ted rolls his eyes.

At that moment I discover what anyone who's taken a ride in the trunk of a limo discovers: there's no graceful way to get out. Scooting on my rear end, I inch towards the light. Once more, I'm beyond grateful that I'm not wearing a dress.

'Julia!' I blurt out, noticing that Julia Roberts is staring

146

at me, too. 'You look awesome. Who are you wearing?'

I reach my hand out of the trunk, but Julia doesn't shake it. Instead, one of the security guards grabs it and yanks me onto the kerb. Ted, ever the gentleman, reaches into the trunk for my backpack, tape recorder and flashlight.

'He had nothing to do with this,' I say. It's beginning to sink in that I may be in trouble and dragging Ted down with me. The celebrity crowd, I notice, has moved away from all the limos.

'Ted didn't know I was in there, did you, Ted?' I say.

Shooting me a peeved look, Ted says, 'No. I didn't know you were in my trunk.'

More wedding-cake dresses and penguin suits have crowded onto the entryway in front of the hotel. Newcomers keep asking, 'What's going on?'

'You can go,' the guard says to Ted.

Ted glances at me once more before he slams the trunk shut and climbs back into the driver's seat. Julia and her entourage are already inside.

'You, young lady, are coming with me.'

Still holding my arm, the guard leads me past the beautiful crowd. Everyone is staring. I'm mortified, bummed beyond beli—

'Toby!'

Without even realising it, my mouth flies open and I frantically wave at Toby Richmond with my free arm.

Toby turns around. The guard stops.

With nothing else to lose, I shout, 'It's me, Susanna Barringer! I work with Sasha at *Scene*. We met in the Admiral's Club in New York. You're wearing Olivier Somebody who has great hair!'

Toby emerges from the crowd like a bud blossoming into a rose.

'Are you being arrested?' he asks, warily.

My face goes pale. *Am* I being arrested?

Stress, humiliation and desperation loosen my lips. There, in front of everybody who is anybody, a gazillion dollars in designer duds, even more in precious jewels, I open my mouth and spill my guts.

'Do you have any idea how hard it is to get a scoop at the Academy Awards?!'

I blather on about losing my pass, about Meryl Gummer and toilet cams. I swear that I'd make an excellent celebrity reporter if I didn't have to spend so much time walking Stella and satisfying Nell's peckishness.

'All I want is a chance to show the world what I can do,' I say. 'Is that too much to ask?'

Toby laughs.

'Right now, miss,' the security guard says, 'you're going

148

back to the press room, where I expect you to stay for the rest of the night.'

'So I'm not being arrested?'

'Not if you behave yourself for the rest of the night.'

I beam. Letting go of my arm, the officer points to Highland Avenue.

'You can't get through the front entrance any more,' he says. 'We'll have to circle around to the back.'

Before following him, I turn to Toby and say, 'Thanks for listening, Mr Richmond. Good luck presenting tonight.'

Then, my head held high, my shoulders hanging on a hanger, I brush carpet lint off my black pants and head back to work.

'Hey, Susan.'

Toby Richmond trots over.

'It's Susanna,' I say.

'I was just wondering, Susanna, do you want a ride?'

TWENTY-FIVE

No way is this happening to me. My mouth is stuck in a goofy grin, my bare toes are tingling. Toby Richmond just invited me into his limo for a ride to the red carpet. In the back seat, not the trunk!

I'm the luckiest girl in the world!

Ted isn't driving this limo. Which is good since he's probably mad at me. Instead, an older man with a perfectly round bald spot pulls up to the hotel's entrance and gets out to open the door for me. For *me*. Will I ever be able to stop smiling?

'Wait a second,' Toby says, as I climb into the air-conditioned back seat of a limousine that looks exactly like ours. Both look way better from the inside.

Toby vanishes into the crowd for a moment, giving me the chance to fluff my hair up and frantically reach into my pack for Chapstick. While I do, I scan for stars. I see Geena Davis and Jamie Foxx. And there's Meryl

Gummer! All are larger than life. It's *so* obvious why they are stars. They are lit from within. Hollywood doesn't anoint just anybody.

'Mind if we add another couple to our carpool?' Toby asks, poking his head through the open door.

'Of course not,' I say, moving over. Then it hits me how truly skanky I must look. I never was able to remove all the carpet lint. And trunk humidity really does a number on curly hair.

'My God,' I gasp.

There he is.

Floating towards me, I see the scar in his eyebrow. His blond hair now brushes his shoulders.

'It's him!' I squeal.

'Do you mind?' Toby asks, jokingly.

I try to answer, but who can talk when Randall Sanders is about to sit inches away from you?

Toby steps away from the door and I hold my breath, waiting for Randall to enter the limo. Instead, a fifty-something woman gets in. She's wearing a black silk gown with a fussy wrap.

Checking out my outfit, she groans. 'God, I wish I was wearing your pants.'

'You look gorgeous, Pauline,' Toby says. 'Meet my friend, Susanna.'

We shake hands as she asks me, 'How did you get out of wearing a designer's ego trip?'

I'm tempted to explain about trunk lint. Instead, I pull my press pass out of my Infinity Edge cleavage-maker and say, 'I'm working.'

Toby says, 'Pauline is Randy's mother.'

'The woman he bought a house for!'

Pauline laughs. 'I like to think of myself as the woman who suffered thirty-two hours of labour to bring Randy into the world, but the house *is* very nice.'

Once again, Toby moves away from the limousine door. This time, my heart stops completely as Randall Sanders steps in.

'Don't I know you?' he asks me.

I try to speak like a normal mortal. Really I do. But my tongue is suddenly flopping around my mouth like a salmon stuck on a rock. All that comes out is, '*Malvee premwehhe and wafta pwarty.*'

'This is Susanna,' Toby says, getting in the car and saving me. 'Our very own reporter from *Scene* magazine.'

'Oh, yes,' Randall says, eyeing me sideways. 'I remember you now. *The Man in the Window* premiere party.'

My heart plummets to my weak knees. He doesn't seem nearly as happy to see me as I am to see him. Before the limo moves, he leans over. I hold my breath and wait for him to reach across my lap, open the door, and kick me out.

'*Cwan we*—?'

That's when it happens.

Randall Sanders plants a kiss on my cheek. A *real* solid smooch with his perfect lips. Not a cheek-brush and air-kiss. Not a dry kiss with pinched lips like your grandmother would give you. Randall leans so close to my face I can smell his citrus cologne. Then he presses two pillowy lips against my cheek. I feel my skin indent. As he pulls away, the imprint remains.

'Thank you,' he whispers in my ear. The warm air from his mouth swirls around the folds of my ear.

'Let's go,' Toby says, knocking on the window that separates the driver from the passengers.

The limo lurches forward. Randall pulls back. He tilts his head up and we lock gazes. In that nano-second, I understand everything. I feel as though I know how the Earth began, how the Universe was formed. I know that the Loch Ness monster is a fake and Big Foot is a hoax. Suddenly, I feel sure I know what happened to Amelia Earhart and the true identity of Jack the Ripper.

At that moment, I understand that Randall Sanders

trusted me last summer to keep his secrets safe. And I did.

'You're welcome,' I say, quite sure my smile will last the rest of my life.

TWENTY-SIX

It's like crossing the finish line at the end of a marathon. People cheer wildly, arms reach out. Giant white lights illuminate the red carpet as we pull up in front of the Kodak Theatre.

Since nobody tells me I can't, I tuck my press pass back into my bra, brush off my black pants, straighten my purple velveteen jacket, and climb out of the limo behind Pauline, Randall and Toby. Uncontrollably grinning, I wave at the crowd.

'Toby! Randall!'

Women shout their names from the bleachers. Pens and autograph books stick out like porcupine quills. I spot the woman in the big glasses from yesterday. She somehow made it into the coveted sideline seats. As I see recognition flash across her face, I wave at her. Dazed, she limply waves back.

When Nicole Kidman passes me, I practically faint. Up close, her skin is so pearly, it's unreal. Same with Kate

Beckinsale, Scarlett Johansson, Reese Witherspoon and Keira Knightley. Don't these women ever get zits?

'Randall! Toby!'

Toby, Randall and Pauline are quickly snatched by publicists. They're led to an *Access Hollywood* reporter and her cameraman. Pauline stands proudly behind her son. Toby grins and socks Randall on the arm. I can't hear what they are saying in the roar of the crowd, but the reporter laughs and they both look so comfortable, it's like standing on the red carpet at the Academy Awards is just another ho-hum day.

'Excuse me.' A different publicist in a black pantsuit approaches me and asks, 'Who are you?'

I laugh.

'Crud, I'm a nobody,' I say, and I walk past her. Down *the* red carpet. Elbow-to-elbow with every star in the world.

It's completely surreal. The lights, the chatter, the air-kisses, the smell of expensive perfume, the soft *whoosh* of satin hems brushing against the carpet, the sparkle of diamonds. Bizarrely, no one pays any attention to me. Even as I wave. Down there, on the RC, it's a square dance. The star sashays out of the limo, hooks elbows with a publicist, is led in front of a TV reporter, twirls in front of a photographer, then two-steps into the theatre, making way for the next star.

Swing thru. Allemande left. Do-si-do.

Ahead, I see that the theatre entrance is a few steps away. I don't want it to end. I long to circle back and start over. *Swing thru.* But, as I turn around, I see there's no going back. The red carpet is a one-way sea of stars – all leading into the theatre where Hollywood's biggest night is about to begin.

'Who are you wearing?!'

My ears hear a familiar voice. It's Joan Rivers! The one woman who isn't afraid to tell it like it is. She gushes, fawns, coos, then she rips a celebrity's outfit to shreds.

In person, Joan is beautiful. Her face looks softer than it does on camera – less surgically redecorated.

'The Gap,' I shout, beaming, as I pass by her.

She laughs. 'Darling, you look fabulous!'

It's over in an instant. The moment I enter the theatre, I'm busted. Again.

'Susanna Barringer?'

A security guard steps forward. He wears a hat and has handcuffs hanging from his belt.

'Yes?' I squeak.

'We're expecting you,' he says. 'Right this way.'

Together, we walk up the grand staircase to the second-floor lobby. I notice that the curtains are indeed closed over the glass wall in front of the 'Tears and Repairs' room. The air is vibrating with anticipation. The stars who are already inside the theatre have gone straight to their seats, or to the bar upstairs. During their acceptance speeches, we'll know who tried to calm their nerves with alcohol.

'How did you know my name?' I ask the guard.

He laughs. 'Everyone knows the name of the kid in the trunk.'

With that, he escorts me to the door leading into the press room.

'I won't see you again, will I?' he says.

'Well, I don't know—'

'That was a statement, Miss Barringer. I won't see you again because you're going to stay where you belong. In the press room with the other reporters.'

'Oh. Yes. No more tricks.'

Besides, I like the sound of that. 'In the press room with the other reporters.' What could be better than that? I, Susanna Barringer, am one of the *reporters*. In the Kodak Theatre. On Oscar night. How lucky can a girl get?

The guard opens the door and I step into the room.

There's an eerie moment of silence as the world's reporters seem to swivel their necks in unison and stare at me. Then they all erupt at once.

'Susanna! Susanna! Miss Barringer!'

'Girl in the trunk!'

My mouth hangs open. I blush purple.

Instantly, I'm in the middle of a feeding frenzy – surrounded by the same group of international reporters that ignored me yesterday and shoved their butts in my face when I tried to reach for a sandwich.

'A quick interview!' someone yells.

'Five minutes!' someone else shouts.

'*Cinco minutos!*' someone calls out in Spanish.

My lips just hang there limply, unable to form any words.

Like a killer whale breaking through the surf, Nell Wickham rises up and struts through the crowd.

'She's not available,' she says.

I'm not? Then I wonder, available for *what*?

'You can read her exclusive in the next issue of *Scene* magazine.'

You can?

The crowd collectively groans. At that moment, an usher from the theatre pops his head through the door and announces, 'The show starts in ten minutes.'

As quickly as it started, my press conference is over. The reporters and photographers return to their positions in front of the winner's stage. Even Nell scurries out to take her seat in the audience.

My fifteen minutes of fame are over in *cinco minutos*.

'You're late,' Keith says, handing me the Polaroid camera.

'I . . . I . . .' I stutter. What can I say?

Keith laughs and loops his arm around my neck. 'You are one gutsy girl, Susanna.'

'Thank you,' I say. 'I think.'

Hanging the camera's strap around my neck, I grab my notebook and pen. One of the foreign photographers reaches up to increase the volume on the television monitor mounted on the wall. My heart pumps overtime as the music swells.

'Ready?' Keith asks.

'I've been ready all my life,' I say.

Standing next to Keith Franklin, in the press room, Polaroid in hand, listening to the start of the Academy Awards, waiting for the first winner to appear, and assigned an exclusive with *Scene* magazine, I feel waves of happiness through my entire body. Who needs a *Limousine Confession* when I'll soon be face-to-face with the best Hollywood has to offer?

'Well, Susanna,' Keith says close to my ear, 'you finally got your scoop.'

I can't stop smiling,

I, girl in the trunk, am the happiest girl in the world.

162

TWENTY-SEVEN

I'm thinking about Mr Pants. He's a dog we used to have who was always excited. He was forever wagging and panting. The mere sound of the cup digging into his sack of dog food created an inner earthquake – he trembled from nose to tail. But the one thing that really sent Mr Pants into a frenzy was the buzzer on our apartment door. Whenever someone came over, they buzzed us from the lobby and Mr Pants went berserk. He did cartwheels and chased his tail.

One Saturday morning, Dad took his coffee into the lobby and stood there, pressing the buzzer. Mom and I were in the apartment. The Trips were yet to be born. The moment he heard the buzzer, Mr Pants went nuts.

As instructed, Mom and I just sat on the couch casually flipping through the newspaper.

Dad buzzed again.

Mr Pants barked.

Again.

He scratched at the front door.

Another buzz.

Mr Pants ran into the living room, panting, as if to say, 'Why are you just sitting there? Someone's at the door!'

Mom and I didn't move.

This went on for about half an hour. Until the sound of the buzzer no longer sent Mr Pants into a tizzy. After that Saturday, the only thing that leapt up when the buzzer rang was Mr Pants' ears.

So, I'm thinking about our old dog as I stand here, in the press room, dizzy from the parade of stars.

When the first winner came through the door, I went berserk. Not externally, but my insides were definitely on tilt. I'd never seen a star so close. I mean, I could smell his cologne. He won Best Supporting Actor. I searched for signs of tears and undereye make-up, but didn't see any.

'I can't believe I'm standing here,' he said. 'I was amazed to even be nominated.'

Of course I frantically wrote his quote on my pad and took a Polaroid, even though everyone knows him. I wanted to have it for myself. To commemorate this awesome event – losing my virginity to Oscar.

When the second winner emerged through the door, I nearly yelped. She was my pick. She's always amazing.

164

And seeing her only three feet away made my heart thump madly in my chest.

'Geez,' she said, holding Oscar up, 'this little guy is heavy!'

Her make-up *did* look freshened up in the 'Tears and Repairs' room. I definitely noticed a new swipe of lipgloss. And even though she'd been sitting on it for at least half an hour, her satin gown didn't have a single wrinkle. She looked like Cinderella on her way *into* the ball.

I snapped another Polaroid. For my collection.

After hour one, my heart calmed down. I stopped imitating Mr Pants. If a star said something funny, or unusual, I wrote it down. But Keith was right – most of them said the same thing over and over. So I stopped wasting paper.

By the time the second hour turned into the third, I began to notice that a lot of actresses have freckles. You can see them even through heavy make-up. One actor looked like he spray-painted a bald spot, and another seemed to be sucking in his gut while he tried to talk to reporters.

'Really, it was an honour just to be nominated,' he said in little puffs.

As time wore on, superstars became stars who became

celebrities who became people with fussy hairstyles and ridiculously expensive clothes.

I became old Mr Pants. Desensitised to the buzz of Hollywood's elite. Keith and I worked in tandem like we were born to be partners.

'I can't believe it,' I say to him, as the room full of reporters grows weary and the show nears its end. 'Corny as it sounds, stars really are just people.'

He laughs. '*Beautiful* people with private chefs, plastic surgeons, facialists, personal trainers, voice coaches, life coaches, decorators, publicists, managers and a whole staff of arse-kissers.'

Plus, I think, they have freckles and bald spots and spare tyres around their bellies. And moms who gave birth one labour pain at a time.

For some reason, this makes me feel great.

TWENTY-EIGHT

'Ted will take you back to the hotel,' Keith says, in the afterglow of Oscar night, as we pack up our gear.

'Hotel?' I ask, agog. 'What about the Governor's Ball? I *vant* to meet *Ah*-nold.'

Keith chuckles. 'Believe me,' he says, 'these parties are no place for kids.'

Hurt, my lip quivers. After all I've been through, how can he call me a kid?

'Sorry,' he says, reading my mind. 'I know you're more grown up than most of the people here.'

I beam.

'Still,' he continues, 'no parties. Nell promised your parents.'

'My parents?'

'Do you think they'd let you fly three thousand miles to get hammered with a bunch of celebrities?'

Well, I *hoped* they had.

Keith says, 'Look, Ted and the limo are yours until

midnight at *least*. Why don't you do a little exploring?'

'Exploring?'

'See Los Angeles from the luxury of a limo. It's the one night of the year when there's no traffic. Everyone is home watching TV.'

At first, I pout. I don't want the night to end – even though *night* has barely begun. I want to see stars in their own habitat. I long to laugh with Meryl over my attempt to be her child.

'Take the limo, Cinderella,' Keith says. 'Have fun. You deserve it.'

Keith plants a kiss on my cheek. I feel its warm imprint. My heart floods with emotion. I want to thank him for all he's done, but saying 'thank you' feels unbearably lame. How can you just *thank* someone for giving you the chance of a lifetime?

'Go,' Keith says. 'I'll see you tomorrow.'

Weighted down with the camera bags, Keith disappears into the crowd. I watch him leave, hoping for a glance backward, a wave, a wink. But all I see is the back of his gorgeous head as he moves on without me.

Unlike New York, which starts to get dark after *Oprah*, the sun is still out as I leave the Kodak Theatre. In the waning light, the golden archway is purple. The red carpet is the deep scarlet of Dorothy's ruby slippers. The crowd has thinned out – only a few stragglers with their autograph books remain.

I take one last look. How could it all be over so quickly? At the same time, I feel as though I've been in California for weeks.

'Would you like to ride in the car or the trunk?' Ted asks, leaning against the limo.

'I'm sorry about lying to you,' I say.

'You should be.'

'If I'd told you what I was planning, would you have let me do it?'

'No. But you still should have told me. I have to work in this town long after you're gone.'

My shoulders sag. I hadn't thought about that. Will Ted's limo now always be checked more carefully than the rest?

'Honestly,' I say. 'I'm truly sorry. Is there anything I can do?'

'Yes.'

'What? Tell me. Anything.'

Ted opens the passenger side of the driver's seat. 'Ride up front with me.'

My eyebrows shoot up.

'You mean it?'

'How am I going to give you Ted's Tour of LA if you're back there in the limo cave?'

I hop in the front seat. Buckle up.

'Before we go,' I say, 'I have two questions.'

'As a reporter or a friend?' Ted asks.

'One of each.'

He looks wary. 'I'm ready. I think.'

'Who was the first star in your limo tonight? I didn't recognise her voice.'

Ted starts the ignition and pulls out onto Hollywood Boulevard. 'I don't remember,' he says.

'How could you forget? She was your first piece of chocolate!'

'Look, Susanna,' Ted says. 'Everywhere a celebrity goes in this town, they are sold out. Waiters eavesdrop on their conversations so they can sell information to the *National Enquirer*. Nurses peek at their medical records, cashiers note what they buy at the supermarket, stalkers peer over their fences. But when someone is a passenger in my limo, they're safe. They can relax. I'll never tell a soul what goes on in the back seat.'

'Not even me?'

'Especially not you.'

Even though I long to make a living spilling a star's secrets, I can't help but admire Ted.

170

He asks, 'What's your second question?'

'Where's the nearest In 'N' Out Burger?'

Leaving Hollywood Boulevard behind, Ted drives straight into the sunset . . . literally. My tour begins on the famous Sunset Boulevard.

'There's Spago,' he says, pointing, 'and Tower Records, where all the musicians hang out. Down there is the Viper Room.'

'*The* Viper Room?'

'The one and only,' Ted replies.

Besides once being owned by Johnny Depp, the Viper Room is *in*famous. Sadly, it's where actor River Phoenix OD'd and lost his life right there on the sidewalk.

'Ahead are two legendary nightclubs,' Ted continues. 'Whiskey a Go-Go, where Jim Morrison and the Doors got their start, and The Roxy, where Bruce Springsteen began.'

Eyes wide open, I stare at the spectacle that is the Sunset Strip. Huge billboards line both sides of the wide street. As the sun fades, neon lights flicker on. But it's nothing like Times Square. Sunset Boulevard has a distinctly Californian feel – laid-back flash. People on the sidewalk seem more interested in checking each other out than looking up at the sky.

171

'That huge pink thing ahead is the Beverly Hills Hotel,' Ted says, continuing the tour.

Okay, now I'm impressed.

Once we enter 'The Hills' my jaw drops instantly. The pink hotel, tucked into gently swaying palm trees, is gorgeous. It's the kind of hotel you just *know* you'll never be able to afford. It looks like you have to get dressed up just to check in.

A few feet beyond the Beverly Hills Hotel, Ted turns left off Sunset Boulevard. Now I see how the other half lives. Or, more accurately, how the other one per cent lives. The mansions of Beverly Hills are enormous cruise ships rising up behind wide green lawns. Some sit behind high fences, others look like huge haciendas with red-tile roofs and verandas, still others resemble museums of modern art with their towering white geometrical shapes.

'Who lives here?' I ask, awed.

'Old Hollywood stars, new producers, music moguls.'

'Everyone in showbiz?'

Chuckling, Ted says, 'All of Los Angeles is in showbiz one way or another. We can't help it. It's in the water.'

The residential section of Beverly Hills ends in a long, skinny park. Unlike Central Park or Riverside Park back home, no one is walking around. Admittedly, it is almost nine o'clock, but this park, it seems, is purely for show.

Who needs a public green when they have wider lawns in their own front yards?

'There used to be railroad tracks along here,' Ted says, as he drives across Santa Monica Boulevard.

'So we're entering the *wrong* side of the tracks?' I ask.

'Hardly,' he says, grinning. Then he turns right onto a street called Brighton, and left onto Rodeo Drive. Immediately, I feel as though I've been airlifted into Richville. The street oozes wealth. Though the sun is now down, the sidewalks and buildings are so white and so brightly lit, it seems like afternoon. There are even people walking around! Ted drives past the most expensive stores in the world – Armani, Hermès, Gucci, Prada. It's Fifth Avenue with palm trees. And, of course, overly tanned women with cantaloupe boobs.

'This place makes me nervous,' I confess.

'Too Stepford?'

'Too *everything*.'

Leaving Beverly Hills, Ted weaves through side streets full of smaller Spanish-style homes. It's the first time Los Angeles actually looks like a normal neighbourhood. I see cars in driveways and families in windows. Coloured flashes of television screens glow through gauzy curtains.

He makes another left, another right, two more lefts and—

'Voilà!' he says. 'The best hamburger you'll ever have.'

Ted is totally right. My In 'N' Out cheeseburger is juicy and messy and the most delicious burger I've ever eaten. It's over too soon – just like my time in Hollywood. The only thing that remains is a drip of secret sauce on my chin, memories to last forever, and, of course, my very own *scoop*.

TWENTY-NINE

THE GIRL IN THE TRUNK
By Susanna Barringer

It was dark. And hot. Exhaust from the limousine's tailpipe filled the stale air with toxic fumes. I was dizzy, near passing out. Still, a reporter has to do whatever it takes to get the story. Which is just what this reporter did. On Oscar night, when all eyes were on the red carpet, two ears were pressed to the carpeted barrier enclosing the back seat of the limo — uncovering how celebrities *really* feel about the biggest night of the year.

I was the girl in the trunk.

Here's the scoop.

First, red carpet couture — the gowns we love to gawk at — are 'suffocating', 'torture', and a 'designer's ego trip'. The last thing an actress wants to do is sit in one all night. The general consensus: they would all rather be wearing jeans. Plus, since Oscar 'night' actually begins in the bright sunlight of an LA afternoon, professional make-up jobs can morph into clown auditions for Barnum & Bailey's Big Top. The goal: get out of the limo, down the red carpet, and into the air-conditioned theatre asap.

The most relaxed stars on the RC are, of course, the men, who barely need to shower. In fact, from my perch beneath the limo's back hood, the cologne was nearly as toxic as the carbon monoxide. Though it *may* have been the 'diamond bodyguards', who tail each celeb like a silent stalker.

Overheard: Drew B. *loves* chocolate dipped in real gold, Jada P. took two hours to get ready, super-polite Owen W. thanked the limo driver twice, and Randall S's mother spent thirty-two hours of labour bringing him into the world. An effort well worth it when Mr Sanders leaned over to the woman who gave him life, kissed her and whispered, 'Thank you.'

Now that's a guy *not only* a mother could love.

Signing off for now. But you never know where I'll hide next. Checked under your bed lately?

Renee, *Scene* magazine's celebrity editor, helped me put the piece together.

'Don't be afraid to exaggerate,' she said. A wise suggestion since I never did get any spice. Nell wanted me to, uh, *exaggerate* even more.

'How do you know Will wasn't calling a lover?' she asked.

'Because he said, "Wave to Mommy and Daddy,"' I replied.

'It could have been code.'

Thank God she didn't push it. Though my article was admittedly tame, Nell published it anyway, because, as she said, 'The trunk is a fresh angle.'

Fresh? I had to laugh. It was the stuffiest stake-out ever.

'How were you planning to get out of the trunk without being seen?' Renee asked me.

Bizarrely, I hadn't planned it that far. Which, according to Nell, meant I had real potential as a reporter. I dove in without knowing how to pull myself out.

Nell. Nell *Wickham*. The woman who's too high and mighty to find her own loo. She said I had potential. Now *that's* the scoop of a lifetime.

THIRTY

My cell has four missed messages. When I check in at lunch, I hear Nell's voice four times.

Beep. 'Susie, it's Nell. Can you pop by the office?'

Beep. 'Nell here. Swing by some time today, will you?'

Beep. 'Good God, Susan. Where are you? Is your battery dead? Call me.'

Beep. 'This is truly annoying.'

Then, nothing. Dead air and a dial tone.

Well, the planets are back in alignment. I've been home from Hollywood for a week, and Nell has again forgotten my name. She's also, apparently, forgotten that I'm in high school and can't ditch class whenever she's feeling peckish.

While I wait for Mel to join me in the cafeteria, I return her call. Carmen puts me straight through.

'Where have you *bean*?' Nell yells into the phone. Her British accent blasts my ear.

'World History and Chromatography Lab,' I say.

'Chroma *what*?'

'I've been in school, Nell.'

'Oh.'

She doesn't say 'Oh' like 'Oh, I made a mistake.' She says it like 'Oh, what an utter waste of time.'

'When will you be out?' she asks.

'Three o'clock.'

Nell sighs. 'That will have to do.'

'Do what?'

'Get to the office as soon as you can.'

'But—'

Too late. Nell already hung up.

When Amelia joins me for lunch, I'm all exasperated.

'Someone needs to tell that woman I don't work for her any more!'

'Nell?'

'Who else?'

We pick up our trays, shuffle through the lunch line.

'It's not that I'm ungrateful or anything. It's just that we're not in Hollywood any more. I have a life! A boring one without a boyfriend, but a life!'

Mel says, 'Before you trot off to your fabbo life, I forgot to ask you, is Reese Witherspoon as short as she looks?'

I laugh a belly laugh. 'Yes. And Kate Beckinsale is unbelievably beautiful, Jennifer Aniston is unbelievably thin, and Patrick Dempsey is unbelievably hot.'

'Is Randall Sanders still your main man?'

'Definitely. That is, until Keith Franklin junks his shallow model obsession and realises that sexual attraction is really all in the brain.'

'Suzanne. Finally.'

Nell flags me into her office the moment I appear at her door. Everyone is there. Keith is wearing black jeans and his purple bandana, Renee's plaid pants are wide and cuffed, Sasha looks amazing in a charcoal-coloured dress with a fur collar, Nell is wearing a deep blue skirt and white cashmere sweater. I walk in wearing last year's Mucks with black tights and a Gap skirt.

What can I say? It was short notice.

'The coverline is "Red Carpet Confessions",' Nell says.

Everybody is standing over a long table full of page proofs. As I learned last summer, the proofs are the mock-ups of the magazine pages before they actually become magazine pages. Nell shows me the upcoming cover. The issue in which *my* by-line will appear.

'Ooh, ah,' I coo, appreciatively. I'd sound more enthusiastic if I hadn't seen all this already. Renee emailed me copies of the page proofs when they first came out. Which was the coolest thing ever. My name in print! I'd thought I'd keel over on the spot.

Now I'm thinking less generous thoughts.

'I can't stay long,' I say, trying to cover my annoyance that Nell made me come all the way uptown to the office when I have tons of homework to do and *Oprah* is airing a show about the latest fashions to make you look thinner. Not that I can afford anything she recommends. Last year, she was all ga-ga over a T-shirt that cost nearly fifty bucks!

'What do you think of "Catwalk Confessions", Sue?' Nell asks.

'Sounds good.'

I sneak a peek at my watch. I also promised my mom I'd be home as soon as possible to help with The Trips' baths. There were two mysterious deaths on the Lower East Side and Dad has to work late.

'I really should—'

Nell hands me an envelope.

'What's this?' I ask.

'Your press credential.'

'For what?'

'For "Catwalk Confessions", of course.'

My pulse accelerates even as my face remains blank.

Nell turns to Sasha and asks, 'Haven't you talked to Sue?'

'Not yet.'

'Talked to me about what?' I ask.

'We want you.'

My heart thumps. 'For what?'

'Fashion Week.'

I blink. Look down at my Gap skirt.

'Are you familiar with Fashion Week?' Sasha asks.

'Isn't it some big fashion show in New York where Gwyneth Paltrow sits in the front row?'

Sasha laughs. 'I guess you could say that. Fashion Week does attract fashion-forward celebs. Twice a year, Fashion Week is a major event in the city. Designers from all over the world present their new lines. Careers are made. Sometimes broken. Models become supermodels. Some even become superstars.'

Nell pipes up, 'Susanna, darling, we want you to cover Fashion Week for *Scene*.'

Did I just hear correctly? Susanna? Darling? *Cover?*

'I don't know anything about fashion,' I say, dumbfounded.

'Yes. We know.' Her left eyebrow cocks at the sight of my outfit. 'Sasha will help you pull yourself together.'

'You'll be our fly on the wall,' Sasha says.

'Fly?'

'You'll infiltrate Fashion Week's Spring Collections and write an exposé for us.'

'Spring? I, uh, have school.'

'The Spring Collections are presented in September.'

'School starts right after Labor Day.'

Nell glares impatiently at me.

Calmly, Sasha says, 'There are enough shows in the afternoon and early evening for you to attend after school. All you need to do is get in, go undercover, and find out what's really happening behind the scenes.'

'That's all?' I swallow. Hiding in a trunk is one thing. Trying to be invisible in a room full of stick-thin models is *quite* another.

'How am I supposed to—?'

'Do you want the job or not?' Nell snaps.

'Yes! Of course. It's just—'

'You, our fearless state-school teen, will figure out a way to make it work,' Nell says with such authority I almost believe her.

Blood is surging through my veins. My heart is doing a rumba. I start imitating Mr Pants. I've never been more excited – or terrified – in my life.

'You've earned it, Susie,' Nell says. 'We're very proud of you here.'

Proud? Of *me*? Nell is awesome. The best! That jerk in Hollywood was a fool to marry that actress. Who could choose fluff over a woman of supreme substance like Nell Wickham? A woman who can run a whole magazine without even messing up her hair? A woma—

'Before you leave, Sue, pick me up a mango smoothie at Jamba Juice, would you?'

In the elevator, on my way down, I'm unable to hold it in any longer. Leaning my head back, I howl.

'Are you all right?' the startled woman behind me asks.

Beaming, I reply, 'Yes. I'm the luckiest girl in the world.'

Move over, models!

Clear the catwalk!

Fashion Week, here I come.

SUSANNA SEES STARS BY MARY HOGAN

Susanna's walking on air. With some nifty self-promotion using a locked box and a key she has managed to win herself a work experience placement at a celebrity news magazine in New York. It's her foot in the door of journalism as well as an opportunity to indulge her serious celebrity obsession.

But the reality of the job is not quite what she expects. The editor, Nell, treats her like a skivvy, personal shopper and all-round dogsbody and the rest of her fellow office workers aren't much nicer. However the job does have a few perks, such as being sent out celebrity-hunting with the hot magazine photographer, and spotting her heart-throb, Randall Sanders. And when she gets the scoop of the summer, finally Susanna has the chance to shine...

ISBN-13: 9781416901570
ISBN-10: 1416901574

THE SERIOUS KISS BY MARY HOGAN

Libby's father is a drunk, her mum wouldn't know the meaning o
home cooking if it landed in her lap and her brother's in trouble with
the police – but none of this matters, as Zack is interested in HER, no
her home-life.

But just as things are working out on the boy front, Libby's family los
their home, and have to move in with her gran. Libby has to start a
new school, give up her plans for Zack, and leave her best frien
Nadine behind. But slowly she discovers there really IS a silver linin
to every grey cloud – and there's plenty to fall in love with in her nev
home: her gran's cooking, the school outsider who stands up to th
bullies, and the deadbeat boy who wants to show her the beauty c
the desert...

ISBN-13: 9781416901402
ISBN-10: 141690140X